A CORPSE AT THE CASTLE

The Highland Horse Whisperer Mysteries, Book 1

R B MARSHALL

Eden Press

For Dancer, the horse of my dreams, who taught me so very much in the too-short time we had together

Find out more about the author and upcoming books online at rozmarshall.
co.uk/books
Get **your FREE starter library**—sign up for my newsletter: rozmarshall.
co.uk/newsletter

ON LANGUAGE AND SPELLING

A NOTE TO MY AMERICAN READERS:

The characters in this book are British, and the heroine is Scottish, so it would seem strange if they spoke American English.

Because of that, the British spelling and grammar used here might appear like spelling errors.

For example: realise (British spelling), realize (American spelling); colour (British), color (American); panelled / paneled; dialogue / dialog and so on.

We also use some words differently (eg our leg wear is trousers, not pants) and have some colourful dialect phrases ('argy bargy', 'lovely jubley') so I've included a **Glossary** at the back which I hope will be helpful.

ABOUT THIS BOOK

A royal castle. A murder. Only one witness: a horse

Horse trainer by day, I.T. consultant by night, Izzy Paterson is a classic nerd who's better with animals than humans.

But when a body is found at the feet of a prize stallion in the Queen's summer castle in the Scottish Highlands, Izzy—and her new friend Craig—are in the wrong place at the wrong time, becoming suspects in the murder.

In the race to clear their names, Izzy has to employ all her horse whispering and computer hacking skills. Can she piece together the clues in time to stop the mysterious killer from striking again?

A CORPSE AT THE CASTLE

CHAPTER ONE

IT's NOT that I'm addicted to coffee. Much.

But with a job that demands early starts, and a body that's more owl than lark, I need caffeine to make me functional in the morning. The stronger the better. Which was why I was standing at the counter of Kaffe Kalista on a Monday morning in May, mainlining the rich scent of coffee beans and waiting impatiently for my triple-shot cappuccino.

The chrome coffee machine in the corner looked like something NASA would use, rather than a tiny café in an off-the-beaten-track Scottish village. With pipes here and gauges there, it gurgled and hissed imperiously, steaming like a shuttle about to launch.

Kalista Dudek, the Polish owner of the coffee shop, would not have won any beauty contests with her lacklustre brown hair, acne-scarred skin and small, hooded eyes. But she obviously had a degree in rocket science.

She manipulated the machine like a pro, turning knobs and levers until it finally submitted and produced the perfect brew which she placed before me with a flourish.

For me, all for me, I thought as the heavenly aroma reached my nostrils. Like I said, *I* don't think I'm addicted. But if there was a seven-step plan for Coffeeholics Anonymous, my colleague and house-mate, Trinity Allen, would have enrolled me before I had time to say, "To go, please."

We'd only been in Glengowrie for three weeks, and I'd already fallen into the habit of coming to the café for coffee as soon as it opened in the morning, before I started working with the horses at Glengowrie Stud.

As I reverentially took my first sip of the foamy brew, a bell over the door pinged, and in bustled two older ladies, both strangely similar.

Each had grey hair regimented in a tight perm, a tweed skirt encasing a shapeless body and eyes that were sharp as a blackbird hunting for worms. The only real difference was their girth—one was stick-thin, the other cuddly in the extreme.

"Edie and Ina Large. Sisters," Kalista whispered to me, then raised her voice. "Good morning, ladies. What can I be getting for you this morning?"

But they were too busy gossiping to notice her. "Did you see him?" the fatter one was saying.

"Aye, aye," replied the other, her head bobbing like a chicken pecking at grain.

"Like one of them body-poppers, all built up with spheroids."

"Aye, body-pumpers on steroids, aye."

The sisters bustled over to a table at the window and sat down, placing their bulging shopping bags in the aisle where anyone could trip over them. "Wonder what he's wanting with herself at the big house?" said the larger Miss Large. Her eyes widened behind their wire-rimmed glasses. "Could he be a giglio, after her ladyship's money?"

"No, a gigolo, surely not?"

"What is this village coming to?" her sister said, peering

over the net half-curtain and staring down the street. "Of course, I'm not incinerating anything, but it *has* been a long time since his lordship died."

With a start, I realised that they were talking about my employer, Lady Letham. I felt a tiny bit guilty, as I'd been wondering what had happened to her husband, but hadn't dared to ask. Lady L had the air of someone who'd been alone for some time, but I definitely didn't see her hooking up with some muscle-bound toy boy. The sisters must surely be mistaken?

Kalista, meanwhile, adjusted the red apron around her waist, picked up her order pad and a pen, and strode over to their table. "Good morning, ladies." She tapped the butt of her biro on the cardboard back of the notepad. "Can I please be taking your order?"

Counting out some coins, I left the money for my coffee by the till, and waved at Kalista as I left. I had my coffee, and all was well with the world.

Or so I thought.

————

FIVE MINUTES LATER, I drove around the final corner, and into Glengowrie's stable yard.

In the passenger seat sat Trinity, clutching her water bottle and looking more like a young Halle Berry than ever, with her pixie-cut hair, sand-coloured skin and delicate features. "I'll just go get Merlin in," she said, and jumped out, leaving me to park the car.

Across an expanse of concrete, a line of stone-built loose boxes faced me, with a hay barn at one end and an L-shaped apartment on two levels—Stables Cottage, which was to be our new residence, if the builders ever finished—at the other end.

Outside the cottage was a huge oak tree with a parking area underneath. I pulled up beside a battered grey pickup, presumably belonging to one of the builders, grabbed my keep-cup and headed for the tack room, my mind running through the list of jobs I had to do today.

I'd only gone two steps when I gasped in fright and almost dropped my coffee. A dark shape loomed towards me from the nearest stable, and my heart leapt into my mouth—at this time of the morning, nobody else should be on the yard.

"Sorry, m'love," said six foot of solid muscle in a black t-shirt and jeans, topped by faded leather chaps. Small brown eyes regarded me below heavy brows, and short cropped dark hair. "I didn't mean to scare you. I was just looking for the manager."

On a dark Friday night in a trendy Glasgow nightclub the chaps might've led me to a different conclusion, but in the context of Lady Letham's stable yard on the outskirts of Glengowrie in the Scottish Highlands, I deduced he was a farrier—a blacksmith of the horsey variety. But not one that I recognised, although that wasn't really a surprise since I was new here.

"It's okay, I just wasn't expecting anyone this early," I said, taking a deep breath to get my heart rate back under control. This must be the 'gigolo' that had got the Misses Large in a stew. Inwardly, I rolled my eyes, then held out my hand. "I'm Izzy. Izzy Paterson, Lady Letham's horse trainer. How can I help you?"

Dainty is not a word my friends have ever used to describe me. Klutz, yes. Even 'bull in a china shop' on occasion when my clumsy gene has been in the ascendant. But, with my hand enveloped in his ham-sized fist, for a few seconds I felt like a size zero supermodel. *That makes a change,* I thought, smiling up at him.

"Richard Mortimer," said Chunk McDunk with a flash of

pearly-whites, while he did a quick up-down, taking in my navy breeches, navy and teal polo top and turquoise gilet.

I may not be a very girly girl, but I'm into my matchy matchy. But this non-girly girl didn't like being objectified, and Richard's brazen appraisal of my figure took him down a notch in my estimation.

"Pleased to meet you, darlin'," he continued, finally letting my hand go. I resisted the temptation to wipe it on the seat of my jods.

As he stepped back, I caught a glimpse of his boots. *Fancy schmancy.* Rather than the sensible working boots I'd have expected from a farrier, they were cowboy boots patterned in black with decorative stitching, made from snakeskin or crocodile skin. With footwear like that, perhaps he had aspirations to be the next John Wayne.

I stifled a smile. He'd struggle if that was the case, for there wasn't much of a range to ride around here, seeing as we were in the foothills of the Scottish Highlands, with more sheep than people per acre, and hardly a cow to be seen. But that was most likely an improvement on his hometown, if I was guessing right from his accent. There were even fewer cows to be found on the streets of London.

A white transit van roared around the corner, causing both of us to turn in surprise. It screeched to a stop under the tree, a bevy of builders spilling out and heading for the apartment before the engine had even stopped turning. It was only then that I realised that the battered grey pickup must belong to Richard. *Guess he didn't ride here on a mustang after all.*

Fishing in his pocket, the wannabe cowboy pulled out a business card and handed it to me, eyebrows raised. "I heard Lady Letham had a new gel working for her."

My face was hidden, as I was looking down at his card. But if he could have seen it, he'd have seen my jaw muscles tighten. *Girl!* Was he blind? My last birthday cake had so many candles it nearly set the smoke alarm off. *Down another notch.* It took a determined effort to relax my expression. I looked up. "Yes. I just started three weeks ago."

"Like mesel' then, eh? I'm new here too." He raised a shoulder. "But you know what they're like in small towns, I'll always be an incomer." He wiped his forehead with the back of his hand. "If I hear right, there's a shortage of good farriers around these parts. So here I am, hoping I can offer my services to Glengowrie Stud. Word is you've some nice horses."

My head jerked up at the clip clop of hooves on concrete. Round the corner came Trinity, leading one of Lady L's young horses, Merlin.

The Man in Black's eyes widened appreciatively at the sight of her, and he turned on the full wattage of his smile. "Morning, darlin'."

Like the yin to my yang, Trinity was petite compared to my leggy frame, had short brown hair compared to my long dark locks, and was a real people person where I preferred animals and computers. "Trinity, this is Richard Mortimer, a new farrier in the district," I introduced them. "Richard, Trinity works with me at the stables here."

Tying Merlin beside his stable door, Trinity stepped closer to us. "Didn't think I'd seen you before." Her face said, *'I'd have remembered'*, even if the words didn't pass her lips.

I looked from one to the other. Richard's grin was even wider, and something sparked in his eyes. "Are you from London?" he asked. "Me, I'm from Barnet."

"South of the river," she put a hand on her chest. "Camberwell born and bred." Then she tilted her head. "But what brought you up 'ere to Scotland? You're miles from home." She seemed genuinely interested in him.

He looked down at her, taking in her jeans, blue t-shirt and ribbed fleece. "I could ask the same of you, darlin'?"

With a laugh, she pointed at me. "Me mate got us the job here."

"An' I came here hoping to get more clients." Richard winked at her. "Talkin' of which," he segued neatly back into his sales pitch, "what say you to this? For my best customers, the shoeing is discounted, and the visits are free." He turned a puppy-dog gaze on me. "Any chance you could put in a good word wiv 'er ladyship for me? Us newcomers should stick together, like?" he added, opening his hands in a supplicating gesture.

Behind his back, Trin gave a thumbs-up. Obviously she was quite taken with him. But something about him was nagging at me; I just couldn't quite put my finger on what it was. Maybe he was just a bit too smooth. I'd had my fill of slime balls when I worked in the city.

"Uh, I'll certainly mention your visit to Lady Letham." I slid his card into my pocket. But if Trinity liked him, then maybe I should give him the benefit of the doubt. I gave him a quick smile. "Now, if you'll excuse me, I need to do Merlin, then I've three other horses to work before lunch." Picking up a grooming brush, I began to brush the black gelding. "But I'm sure Trinity would be more than happy to show you back to your car," I added, hoping Trin would take the hint.

As they walked away, I could hear Richard's voice rumbling like an ominous thundercloud. "Trinity. Now ain't that a lovely name?"

Hands on my hips, I stared after them. Trinity's attention was on whatever he was saying, a smile playing on her lips.

It seemed like the flirtatious farrier had all the patter, but I could only hope there was more to him than that, because I didn't want Trinity's feelings to be hurt. Again. After the terrible time she'd had in London, she deserved better.

———

BY THE TIME Trinity had seen Richard off the premises, I was already in the round pen with Merlin, leading him around the post and rail enclosure and sending out calming vibes to get him into the right frame of mind for today's training session.

One of the reasons I'd got the job with Lady Letham was because I've qualifications in Horsemanship—the training of horses using 'natural' methods such as body language. Made famous by an American who tamed a wild mustang right off the prairie, we sometimes get called 'horse whisperers', but that's mainly because the things we do are often so subtle they're invisible to the human eye. Personally, I prefer the term 'horse listeners'.

Today, all I had planned for Merlin was to teach the youngster to lead quietly and take his confidence from his handler. It would stand him in good stead later in his career as a dressage horse, when he'd have to contend with unfamiliar surroundings and crowds of people.

Trinity knew better than to interrupt, which would break the horse's concentration. But I could see she was itching for a chat, so when Merlin needed a stretch and a break, I stopped at her side of the pen.

"What did you think of *him*, then?" she asked, without beating around the bush.

"The farrier?" I wrinkled my nose. "Not my type. But I think he liked you."

Her eyes sparkled. "It's just nice that someone eligible has come here. From what I've heard, all the local guys disappear off to Dundee or Aberdeen for work. And it was nice to hear a familiar accent." Then her gaze darted across to the big house. "D'you think Lady L might switch to using him?"

I pursed my lips. "She strikes me as someone who's fairly set in her ways."

Trinity's face fell.

"But we could maybe try him on one of the youngsters. Can't do too much wrong with a trim."

"True!" She assessed Merlin's feet. "But they're not due for a few weeks yet."

I gave her a rueful grin. "Sorry. You'll just have to be patient!"

Her face took on a mischievous look. "Or pray for mud to pull some shoes off!"

I raised my eyes heavenwards. With a new boss to impress and four horses to train, that was the last thing I needed.

CHAPTER TWO

WHEN IT CAME time to ride Leo, my dressage horse, our hack in the countryside didn't go quite as planned.

I'd been blithely enjoying the sunshine and the pastoral views around me, laughing at fluffy lambs playing games of tag while their mothers dreamily munched on lush spring grass. Overhead, chattering swallows swooped and swirled, and the dew adorning the cobwebs on the fence beside the track sparkled like diamonds on a lace bodice.

In the distance, lumpy green hills led steadily northwards towards the barren purple grandeur of the Cairngorm mountains. It made London seem like an overwrought, self-important hell-hole in comparison. I gave silent thanks, once again, that Lady Letham had taken a chance on me, which allowed me to leave all that behind and return to my native Scotland.

And then I spotted something white under a bush.

For someone as tall as me to reach into the small space under the spiky hawthorn bush was really difficult. Especially wearing stiff riding boots, which aren't really designed for scrabbling around on the ground. But it would be worth the scratches if I could just get the little dog—for that's what the white thing turned out to be—to come to me.

It was some sort of terrier, a grubby white and brown thing, with its shoulders stooped and its head hanging, crouching under the prickly shrubs that lined the path I'd been riding along a minute earlier.

"Here, boy, you look like you need a friend," I crooned to the dog, trying to give off an air of kindness. *If I could only stretch a little further, I might reach him.*

Just at that point, Leo helpfully decided to take a step backwards, straining my muscles almost to breaking point. Giving the reins a tug, I clucked at the horse. "Walk on," I asked, and, with the resulting loosening of the reins, I was able to let the dog sniff my fingers.

My reward was a quick lick from a small, pink tongue. "Aw, you're a sweet one," I said. "How come you're out here on your own. Are you lost?"

Could he have strayed while on a walk? I slid a finger down the soft curve of his neck. No collar. *Perhaps he was abandoned deliberately.* That thought made me feel sorry for him, and I extended my hand to pat his head, imagining grey cars and black tarmac and dark skies. "Poor boy."

Beside me, Leo stretched his big face down to look under the bush, and snorted at the little pup.

The terrier's eyes widened in fright, and before I could do anything about it, he'd turned tail, wriggled through a gap, and disappeared off into the trees.

I stared at the black space where he'd been, then scrambled up and turned to Leo with my hands on my hips. "Look what you did! You acted like a fire-breathing dragon and scared him away." Leo, of course, was totally oblivious to what he'd done. His soft brown eyes regarded me calmly, then he moved his attention to the bush beside us, and nibbled at a leaf.

A minute later I was back in the saddle, trying to damp down my frustration and get back to enjoying my ride. Trotting along the path—a disused railway line, now given over to ramblers and horse riders—my eyes scanned from side to side like a spectator at a tennis match, looking for the wee dog. But there was no sign of him. *Maybe I'll find him in the village.*

Our route looped invitingly round a little wood, then led into the outskirts of Glengowrie, the Scottish village that was my new home.

Parked on the verge beside the first cottage we reached was a red van, engine running and indicators flashing orange. A short, wiry man in a dark uniform jacket, blue shorts and running shoes stepped out of the vehicle, tucking a parcel under his arm. "Morning," said the postman, his tanned face crinkling like a walnut as he eyed my chestnut steed. "Is it you that's the new girl who works with the horses at the big house?"

"Yes." It would never cease to amaze me how quickly gossip could get round a small village. "I'm Izzy Paterson. Nice to meet you."

"Evan Grainger," said the postie, who positively bristled with energy. "Tidy horse you've got there."

"Thanks." I smiled at him. "Oh—you've not seen a wee white and brown terrier on your rounds today, have you? A Jack Russell, I think. Or did you hear if anyone has lost a dog? I saw him in the wood back there," I indicated over my shoulder, "but he ran away before I could catch him."

Evan shook his head slowly. "Not that I can recall." His face brightened. "But if I hear anything, I'll be sure to let you know."

———

TRAINING AND RIDING FINISHED for the morning, Trinity and I were grabbing a quick bite to eat in the tack room before starting the afternoon's work. There was something comforting and old-fashioned about the smell of leather and saddle soap, the worn oak boards on the floor, and the soft grey light filtering through the small panes of the ancient window.

Her knife poised over a jar of apple chutney, Trin frowned at her sandwich. "I wonder what *really* brought him up here from London?"

My head had been full of the morning's work, making mental notes of what to do next with the horses, so it took me a minute to realise she was talking about Richard the farrier. I blinked. "I dunno. Unless he trained up here."

"But he must've been working for a while—he ain't that young. Thirty? What d'you think?"

Trin was a little older than me, with the big three-zero approaching fast, and she was a bit touchy about her age. After a disastrous relationship in London, an eligible man of a similar age was exactly what she needed.

However, Trin's question helped me realise what had been bothering me about the Lonesome Cowboy. *Why would a decent farrier uproot himself, leave his clients and his friends and start anew in a place like this?* Glengowrie was lovely, but it wasn't exactly the centre of the universe.

Of course, you could ask the same question about me, but in my case I left a totally different career in the rat race of London to pursue my dream of being a dressage rider and trainer. Lady L was the first person to take a chance on me— so here I was, back in my native Scotland and loving every minute of it.

Plucking a couple of grapes from the bunch in the fruit bowl, I leaned back. "At least thirty, I'd say. You'll need to ask him more about his background, next time you see him."

Trinity's face brightened at the thought. "I'd better start doing a rain dance," she said with a mischievous glance at me.

Oh dear. She really is smitten.

I was spared from any more musings about the new farrier by the entrance of Lady Letham, resplendent in cashmere and floral print, randomly accessorised with red gardening gloves, green wellies, and a polka-dot patterned walking stick. "I come bearing gifts!" she said, leaning on her stick with one hand, and setting a round tin filled with sugar-sprinkled shortbread on the table between us. "Or," she paused, "should that perhaps be bribes?"

An index finger raised imperiously. "But first, lest I forget, the plumber is scheduled to do the last few..." her fingers waved in the air, "thingummy-bobs on Stables Cottage next week. So you should be able to move in the following weekend."

The cottage at the top of the stable yard should actually have been ready when we first started at Glengowrie Stud. But it seemed that project management wasn't Lady L's foremost skill. "Thank you, we'll look forward to that," I said, waving a hand at an empty seat. "Please, sit down. Have some shortbread."

"Don't mind if I do." She propped the stick against a wooden saddle rack and delicately picked up a biscuit. "I'll tell Jacintha that you'll be moving from her pied-à-terre in town, forthwith."

Trinity raised an eyebrow. "It'll be good to get me own room again. And not have to wear earplugs."

I gave her an evil look. She insisted that I snored, but I was convinced it was just heavy breathing that was amplified in the quiet of night.

"Oh, I do apologise most profusely, my dear." Lady Letham brushed some sugar crumbs from her skirt, then gave

Trinity a placatory look. "Jacintha's place was the only one available at such short notice."

"It's been fine," I said, anxious not to upset my employer. "But we'll look forward to being here on site. It'll be better in case of any emergencies. Now, you said something about a favour?"

Lady L caught my eye and clasped her hands together. "Yes. Isobel, darling, I have a special task for you. I've just been on the telephone to my dear friend Libby, and I've organised for the big girls to go up and meet her handsome boy Eagle. If all goes well, we'll get some little Eaglet babies in eleven months' time."

"Allegra and Daisy?" I asked, translating her shorthand to mean that she wanted her two warmblood mares to go to stud where a stallion would have his wicked way with them.

"Yes. Eagle is such a gorgeous Highland Pony. You know that my ambition is to breed some of the best Scottish Sports Horses. I'm sure that, with his bloodlines, he'll produce some lovely foals."

"Okay." I bit one of the grapes in half, savouring the sweet taste. "When do you need them to go?"

She pushed the tin of biscuits in my direction and gave me a sideways look. "This afternoon, if you could possibly manage that, my dear? I would love for them to get into foal this month, so they will have their foals next April. I think they've both just come into season."

I blinked, mentally reviewing my 'to do' list for today. With eight horses to look after and a part-time business on the side, there wasn't a lot of spare time for unplanned trips. "Where abouts is Eagle?" Maybe if it wasn't too far, I could squeeze it in later this afternoon.

"At Libby's stud," Lady L said, as if everybody should know.

Munching another grape, I creased my brow. "Remember, I'm not from round here."

"Oh yes, dear, of course." She pointed vaguely out the window. "It's north of here. Balmoral. I'd imagine it'll take you at least an hour to get there with the lorry—the roads are just shocking. Single track with passing places for much of the way."

"Balmoral?" Trin interjected. "Like, the Queen's summer palace?"

"Castle," Lady Letham corrected. "Yes. Libby has a stud in the grounds."

"Libby..." My mouth hung open. "You mean, Queen Elizabeth?"

She nodded. "Yes, Libby. That's what I said."

Trin's eyes were like saucers. "You know the Queen?"

"Yes. Ever since I was a girl. In the summer holidays, Mummy would take me up there and we'd play together. Libby, dear Margaret—God rest her soul—and I." As she talked, Lady L's fingers waved through the air, like she was conducting an invisible orchestra. "And then, for a while, I was a lady-in-waiting. That was before I got married to his lordship. Such fun! Travelling the world, the parties, the dresses, the jet-set..." Her face sparkled with the memories.

I swallowed and looked down at my riding breeches and gilet, which had seen better days. *Might have to dig out my best show gear to visit a royal castle.* "Will the Queen be there?"

Lady Letham let out a trill of laughter. "No, no, she won't be there till the summer. Dear Libby is at Windsor just now, hosting a reception for an ambassador or some such. You'll be seeing her man, Hamish. Hamish Douglas, who runs the stud. He's expecting you."

———

WITH MY PRECIOUS cargo of Lady Letham's two best mares
in the back of the lorry, I negotiated the last few miles to
Balmoral on autopilot while I went over the arrangements—
and rearrangements—we'd had to make to accommodate this
unexpected trip, to make sure I'd not forgotten anything.

Around me, imposing pines crowded either side of the
narrow road that followed the route of the River Dee. On
one side, the land fell away and down to the tumbling river,
although I only got glimpses of it through the trees. On the
other, rolling hills and forests led north and west to the
majestic mountains of the Cairngorms National Park. But,
for once, the soaring landscape didn't soothe my mood.

It wasn't the first time in the last three weeks that Lady L
had sprung something unexpected on me. I hadn't worked
out yet if she was spontaneous or just disorganised. *Perhaps the
latter.* Surely she must've been planning to send the mares to
stud for a while? It's not something you just do on the spur of
the moment.

Or maybe she'd always intended to send them to
Balmoral, and just forgotten to tell me? *That's probably more
likely.* She did say she'd just noticed that the mares had come
into season. And at her age, forgetfulness probably went with
the territory.

A sign up ahead had a castle on it and an arrow pointing
right. Crunching the lorry down a gear, I turned into tourist
car parks milling with spring visitors to the castle, thinking
about how I'd have handled a boss like this during my time at
the bank.

I'll ask her to have a weekly planning meeting. And I would use
that time to report back on the youngsters' progress and
discuss any competitions we could enter. *Yes, that might work.*

Hopefully, that way I'd not get any more surprises sprung
on me, and have to leave Trinity to cope on her own. *Well,
almost alone.* Lady L had asked Jimmy, her handyman, to do

some extra hours to help while I was away. Jimmy was a hard worker, and would muck out four boxes in the time it took me to exercise one horse. But he didn't take anything directly to do with the animals. So Trin would be left with all the rugging, grooming and turnout to do by herself.

And I wasn't going to be away just for an afternoon, as I'd originally thought. Lady L had asked me to stay till the morning, so I could be sure the mares were settled before I came back. I glanced at the small bag on the passenger seat, which contained my overnight stuff and my laptop. *At least I can get some work done this evening at the B&B.* So the trip wouldn't be a total bust.

"After one hundred yards, you have reached your destination!" the sat-nav pinged as we crossed an iron-balustraded bridge over the river.

Up ahead on the right I could see imposing wrought-iron gates set into a granite-block wall beside a modest, stone-built gatehouse. A policeman stood guard.

We're here, I thought, straightening my spine and gripping the steering wheel. The queen might not be in residence, but it was still a daunting place to visit. I could only hope that Hamish the stud manager would be friendly.

CHAPTER THREE

IT WASN'T HAMISH that I met first, though. Searching for something that looked like a stable yard, I eased the truck along one of the back roads in the Balmoral estate, wishing I'd not been too intimidated to ask the security guard for directions.

Ahead of me was a guy in green wellies, cord trousers and green tweed jacket, striding along the side of the road with a black Labrador at his heels. The only thing that spoiled the *Monarch of the Glen* look was a rather incongruous faded blue baseball cap on his head. Unruly reddish-brown curls escaped from the bottom and spilled over his collar.

"Excuse me," I called, pulling alongside him and winding down the window. "I'm looking for Hamish at the stables."

The green eyes he turned on me were arresting, that was the only word for it. They were offset by a chin with slightly too much scruff on it, a high forehead and a wide mouth. *How would I describe him to Trin?* Somewhere between boy-next-door and Hollywood, maybe? *Yeah.*

Pushing the brim of his hat up his forehead, he gave a wry

smile. "If you're looking for the stables, I'm afraid you're headed the wrong way."

His voice wasn't the Hooray Henry received pronunciation I'd expected from his garb. Instead, he spoke with a soft Highland brogue—presumably a local.

For a moment, he stared down the road behind us, then seemed to come to a decision. "But I can show you, if you'd like?"

———

"I'M CRAIG MACDONALD," he said as he clambered into the passenger seat, encouraging his dog to sit between his boots in the footwell, "and this is Jet." He held out a hand. "Welcome to Balmoral."

"Thanks," I replied. "Izzy Paterson." His strong masculine presence, the faint aroma of sandalwood and the brief clasp of his warm hand momentarily froze my brain. It was a while since I'd been near a man my own age. *Obviously. Get a grip, Izzy.*

I cleared my throat. "Usually I'd look up Google Maps or get instructions, so I know where I'm going. But my boss was rather vague, and I guess even Google gets their wrists slapped if they provide too much detail of where the royals live."

He chuckled. "Aye, and thon's only the half of it. Did they make you sign away your firstborn just to get through the gate?"

"Pretty much."

Circling a finger in the air to indicate I should do a u-turn, he nodded at the visitor pass on the dashboard. "And it'll be the same rigmarole all over if you come back here again." He pierced me with those emerald-green eyes. "Or is this just a one-off visit?"

For a minute, I concentrated on manoeuvring the lorry into a rather ungainly thirteen-point turn. It gave time for my heart rate return to normal. "I'm not sure, to be honest. I'm delivering a couple of mares to the stud and I've to check on them tomorrow. I guess I'll need to collect them at some point if they've to stay—Lady Letham was a bit vague on the details."

"Of course! So old Alice is your boss." There was a brief pause, then he quirked an eyebrow. "But that would explain a lot." He pointed into a small side road. "Turn left here."

"Oh dear. Is there something I should know? About Lady Letham, I mean. I've not worked for her very long."

He smiled, revealing teeth that were also somewhere between Hollywood and Haddington. *Not perfect. But not bad.* "Och, don't worry. She's no' an axe-murderer or anything like that. Just a bit... forgetful."

"Phew!" I hammed it up, wiping my brow theatrically.

"And turn right at this one," he directed. "So I'm guessing you're new here?"

"Yeah. Just moved three weeks ago. I'm from just outside Edinburgh, but I don't know this area of Scotland at all."

Up ahead on the left of the road I spied two grey stone cottages with slate roofs, white porches, and gardens which seemed to be competing to be the most colourful. Beyond them was a parking lot, then a riding arena with a crumbed rubber surface, surrounded by a post and rail fence. A building along one side of the arena formed part of a square stable block, with a clock tower over the open gates directly ahead. "Is this us?"

"Aye." He nodded at the arched entrance. "Drive on in and you can unload inside."

I stopped the lorry near the top of the large, extremely tidy, stable yard. *Guess the Queen likes things to be pristine.* The cobbles were swept within an inch of their lives, so clean that

I could probably eat my dinner off them. This was most likely thanks to a poker-thin man over in the corner who was wielding a broom like it was an Olympic discipline. Everything else in the yard was grey granite or wood, painted gloss black.

Craig opened the passenger door and stepped down. "Well, it was nice to meet you, Izzy, I'll leave you now. Me and Jet will carry on our walk from here."

"Are you sure? I can give you a lift back if you wait till I've sorted the girls."

"There's no need—the woods are just up there." He indicated a gap in the stable block ahead of us, then raised a hand in farewell. "Good luck."

"Thanks." Then I frowned. *Why would I need luck?* I stared at his retreating back, before jumping out of the cab myself. *Maybe he's just being polite.*

———

TURNS out Craig wasn't just being polite. Hamish Douglas was a piece of work.

With wiry grey hair and a red-veined nose, he came bustling over as I walked Allegra down the ramp, his pudgy eyes practically bulging out of his head. "You can't unload here!"

I looked around me, perplexed. Where else was I supposed to unload the horses?

Perhaps he thought I was making the place look untidy. What was that old joke? That the Queen thought everything smelled of new paint as everyone redecorated before she visited? It must make her staff somewhat OCD.

Giving myself a mental shake, I gave him my best fake smile and raised a shoulder. "I'm sorry, someone told me to unload here, and the mares are off the lorry now. Surely you don't want me to re-load them?" I added sweetly and held out a hand. *Better try to get on his good side.* "I'm Izzy Paterson. Lady Letham sent me with her two mares for Eagle."

Briefly, his eyes turned into slits, then he grunted and tilted his head to the right. "Over here," he said, ignoring my hand, and marched off.

Leading the two mares, I followed him through a gap on the right side of the yard and down a short laneway leading to fields where various horses grazed contentedly.

Reaching an empty paddock, he opened the gate and jerked his chin. "Leave them here."

Giving the girls a pat, I let them loose in turn, and they trotted off to explore their surroundings. "The bay is Allegra," I said, still trying to smooth the water, "and the grey is Daisy. They're no bother," I added, looping their head collars over the gate.

That got me another grunt.

Oh dear. Had he got out of the wrong side of the bed this morning, or did he have chronic people issues? Then I remembered Craig's 'good luck' comment, and my heart sank. It was probably the latter.

Since I was likely to be dealing with him regularly, I needed for us to get along, or at least be civil. Except, I wasn't exactly the best with people either. I wracked my brains. What would someone gregarious like Trinity do?

Inspiration struck, and I turned my best smile on him, hoping a charm offensive would break down some of his barriers. "Might it be possible to meet Eagle, if you could spare a minute?"

He narrowed his eyes at me.

Before he could find some way to refuse, I added, "I've a mare myself," well, I would have in the future, if my plans worked out, "that I might put in foal. It would be good to meet him when he's not—uh—working."

Boxed into a corner, he glowered, then turned and stomped off. "This way," he threw over his shoulder.

As we were crossing the cobbled yard, a green jeep came swinging through the entrance, driven by a guy wearing similar huntin' shootin' getup to Craig. In my experience, it tended to be a bit of a dress code with the country fraternity.

To my surprise, Hamish MacGrumpy stopped in his tracks, and the corners of his mouth turned upwards. Slowly, granted, like they needed oiled, but it was definitely a smile. Of sorts.

The lanky figure that unfolded himself from the utilitarian vehicle reminded me of the child catcher in Chitty Chitty Bang Bang—all nose and angles. "Douglas, my man," he said with a tight smile, "just came to tell you we'll be five for the shoot tomorrow. So two ponies perhaps?"

"Aye, sir." Hamish all but tugged his forelock. "I'll get the boy to have them ready at nine o'clock sharp."

I had a hard time stopping my jaw from hitting the ground. Was this really the same guy who'd practically bitten my head off?

"Excellent," the tall man replied, then clambered back into his jeep and drove off in a cloud of exhaust smoke.

As soon as the other man disappeared, Hamish was back to Mr Congeniality mode. The lines on his forehead matched the horizontal line of his mouth as he jerked his chin at a stable ahead of us. "That's 'im. Lochnagar Golden Eagle." Briefly, his eyes softened; so briefly I thought I'd imagined it.

Over the half-door, gentle brown eyes perused us. The stallion was a glorious fawn colour, glinting like gold in the sunlight. His mane and forelock were black, providing a stunning contrast with the metallic hue of his coat.

"He's gorgeous!" Offering my hand for him to sniff, I let him get used to my scent, then rubbed his noble nose. "Good boy," I crooned.

With a sniff, Hamish turned and shouted at the man with the brush. "Stan!"

There was no reaction; Stan just kept on sweeping, hard and fast, like he was trying to guide a curling stone to the bullseye.

"Deaf as a post," Hamish muttered, and tried again. This time he positively hollered, "Stanley Fisher!"

It did the trick, because Stan jumped in surprise, then leaned the broom on the wall and came across to join us. He had the most curious gait—he almost slid across the yard, with no appreciable bounce to his steps. His appearance was also very strange, with thin, light-coloured hair, pale skin, a long face, small eyes and thin nose. He had something of a ghostly air about him. *Creepy.*

"Get Eagle out," Hamish instructed, his voice a decibel or two above normal.

No obvious emotion crossed Slytherin Stan's face as he unhooked a head collar from the wall beside the stallion's stable, fastened it on, then led the horse out into the yard. But there was a flicker of something in his pale eyes—*resentment, maybe*—and his gaze darted back to his brush in the corner of the yard. Perhaps Stan was the OCD one who kept the yard looking pristine, and we were messing up his pride and joy.

Hamish spent a minute getting Eagle to stand with his feet parallel, so that he'd show himself to the best advantage, then gave him a quick pat on the neck. He obviously knew his stuff. No wonder the Queen had him on her staff. Even if he *was* a grumpy so and so.

Walking a circle around the stallion, I checked out his well-muscled back and unblemished legs. "Very nice." Straightening, I decided to push my luck. "Could I see him move?"

That earned me some side-eye from the crotchety stud

manager, but a flick of his finger was enough to have Stan lead the horse through the little corridor leading to the outdoor school.

A few minutes later, after watching him walk and trot round the arena, I was even more impressed by the stallion. *No wonder Lady Letham chose him.* "Thank you. He would definitely make a very nice sire for my mare." I crossed my fingers behind my back. *My dream future mare.*

Nodding his acknowledgement, Hamish jerked his chin at Stan to put Eagle away again, then pointed at a black-painted door on the other side of the passageway leading to the outdoor arena. "Bring the mares' passports," he instructed, and stomped off without waiting for me.

A couple of minutes later I was standing in front of his desk while he laboriously transcribed information from Allegra and Daisy's horse passports into a large leather-bound ledger. It felt like being in the headmaster's office at school, dreading the thought of detention.

While I waited, I looked about me. Hamish might be dour as a wet Wednesday, but he was obviously meticulous. Or ex-military. Everything had a place, and mostly that place was on a shelf or in a drawer or filing cabinet. His desk was empty apart from the paperwork in front of him, an old computer angled towards him on the left, and a wooden 'in' tray by the right-hand corner.

The walls were covered with oak-framed photos of horse show successes, shooting parties, and middle-aged men in suits. In one of those, Hamish was standing proudly in the centre wearing a gold chain, a purple tartan sash and bonnet, and carrying a staff. I frowned. He didn't strike me as enough of a people-person to be a councillor or mayor. *Strange.* People were surprising.

Setting his pen down and pushing the passports towards

me, Hamish glanced up. "Come back tomorrow at ten. Stan will be here to help, and Eagle will service them then."

Then he set the ledger aside, pulled a letter from the in-tray, and opened it with a letter-opener that looked remarkably like a jewelled dagger. Perhaps it had been a present from the Queen? Pulling a pair of half-moon reading glasses from his pocket, he started reading.

After waiting a moment longer, I realised he had nothing else to say. *Guess that's me dismissed then.* Picking up the passports and slipping them into their protective sleeve, I turned and made my way back to the lorry, shaking my head. Tomorrow was obviously going to be a barrel of laughs.

––––––

PULLING THE LORRY—MY only mode of transport—up outside of the B&B, I killed the engine and sat for a minute staring at the architectural marvel before me, and wondering what I'd got myself into.

The website had said 'the best B&B for Balmoral'. It had omitted to mention that it was the *only* guest house within fifteen miles of the castle which I guess also made it the worst...

White stone cladding adorned the front wall of the bunga-low, the rest of which was pebble-dashed in that fawn brown so loved by builders. All very well, but the local stone was grey granite, so it stood out like a sore thumb beside its neighbours.

'Easy care' probably defined the front 'garden', which was cobbled in red. White planters overflowed with garish flow-ers, and plastic dwarves did unmentionable things with fishing poles.

Hefting my overnight bag, I sighed and stepped out of the cab. *Beggars can't be choosers.* At least it looked clean.

Throwing the front door wide, Mrs Beaton welcomed me, all lipstick and costume jewellery. "You'll be Lady Letham's groom."

"Her horse trainer, yes," I corrected.

"We've kept you the best room," she gushed, heels tap-tapping as she led me along a corridor floored with orange-pine laminate. "Her ladyship must be so pleased to have someone reliable. The last girl..." she shivered, raising her palms, then gave me a sharp-eyed look. "Let's just say, the less said the better."

At the end of the hall, the dining room door was open, showing an expanse of paisley-patterned carpet and a view through sliding French doors out to the rear garden. It was a mirror of the front, apart from the addition of a plastic pond with a stone frog in the centre, water jetting from its mouth into the air. *Nice,* I thought. Did I mention that irony is my middle name?

By this time, Mrs Beaton had reached my room, and ushered me into a space that was a symphony of lace and froufrou. I arranged my mouth into a smile. "How lovely," I lied.

"I thought you'd like it." The proprietress turned earnest eyes on me. "Now, if there's anything I can do to help...?"

Quickly, I scanned the room, looking for anything vaguely technical. The TV remote was all I came up with. "You could let me know the wi-fi password? I've some work to do before I go out."

Mrs Beaton reached for the dressing table, then handed me a chintzy flower ornament which held a little card with hieroglyphics printed on it. The password, presumably. "Out?" She raised her painted brows.

"For dinner."

"Oh, of course. You'll want The Queen's Arms then." She nudged my elbow. "Serves a delicious steak."

I sucked air through my teeth. "Unfortunately, I'm vegetarian."

She deflated, like someone had pricked her with a pin. "Oh. One of those," she said, like it was a disease. Shrugging, she opened her palm. "I think they do salads."

Great. How original. I managed not to roll my eyes.

"So," she pinned me with a beady gaze reminiscent of a magpie with something shiny in its sights, "I hear you arrived at Glengowrie with a girl *friend.*" She emphasised the last word, then stopped talking, obviously waiting for me to clarify.

For a moment, I considered leading her on, telling her that Trin and I were getting married next month, or some such nonsense. But I had a feeling that such a tactic would backfire, and that the gossip mongers would have such a glorious tidbit spread from Aberdeen to Aberdour before I'd had a chance to set the record straight.

People tended to be more old-fashioned in the Highlands, so the truth seemed like a better idea than messing with her head. "Yeah, Trinity and I are good friends; we met in London at the stables where I kept my horse. She works as groom and looks after the horses while I get on with the training. I couldn't run the business without her, she's a great asset." Hopefully that would be enough to squash any rumours.

"Ah." Mrs B looked unconvinced. "Yes." She smoothed her skirt and changed the subject. "So, breakfast is any time from seven."

I nodded. "Seven will be good."

"And will you be having the full Scottish? Sausage, bacon, black pudding——"

I raised a hand to interrupt her, refraining from reminding her about the no meat thing. "Just porridge. And maybe scrambled eggs if you have them?"

"Of course." She almost looked offended. "We aim to cater for all tastes at Riverside Guest House."

Putting my bag down, I gave her a sugary sweet smile. "Thank you. I'll look forward to it." Hoping she'd take the hint, I pulled out my laptop and set it on the bed.

She turned for the door. "I'll get you a key, in case you're out after nine tonight."

"Oh, don't bother," I waved a hand airily, switching my computer on, "I'll not be late."

Famous last words.

CHAPTER FOUR

WITH THE NOSY landlady finally out of the way, I sat on the bed and pulled my laptop onto my knee.

Piggy-backing on the B&B's wi-fi, I put the computer into stealth mode, and created a private tunnel to the internet.

It was time to switch my brain into work-mode. I flexed my fingers. *Time for some hacking.*

So, I think I forgot to say. This is my other skill. I'm not the girl with the dragon tattoo—I've no ink—but my job at the bank wasn't to do with finance, at least not directly.

Instead, when I worked for BleuBank, I was in charge of website security. Or, more appropriately, website *insecurity*. My job was to probe for weaknesses and try to hack into our systems. Along the way, I picked up some useful skills, including how to search the hidden parts of the internet—the deep web—for facts people would rather keep secret.

And, now that I'd left London, I hoped those skills would provide some useful part-time income, which I would salt away for a rainy day.

I checked my watch. *Good.* I had a couple of hours until

it'd be time to eat. Plenty of time for my latest assignment. Sinking back into the lace-edged pillows, I set to work.

———

"Izzy!" said a male voice. "Blow me, I never thought to see you again so soon. Is there anyone sitting 'ere?"

Surprise jerked my head up from the menu I'd been perusing. I'd come to The Queen's Arms as Mrs B had said it was the best place to go for my evening meal. The fact that it was the *only* place serving dinner in the tiny village may have had something to do with that...

The Arms had a homely feel, and, even as a woman on her own, I felt safe here. It might have been all the wood panelling, or the log fire flickering in the grate, or the subdued lighting. Whatever it was, it just seemed cozy. But being new to the area and miles away from Glengowrie, I hadn't expected to meet anyone I knew.

Without waiting for an answer, Richard Mortimer slid sideways onto the turned-wood bar stool beside me, like an oil tanker berthing at harbour. A waft of cheap aftershave almost made my eyes water, and this time he had added a black leather waistcoat and stetson to his black ensemble. "Oh, hello," I said, innate politeness doing its thing.

The man in black held up a finger to the barman. "Pint o' Guinness, Zak, mate, when you've got a minute." He turned to me. "And something for the lady?"

Oh, I'm a lady now, not a girl? Perhaps the sliver of make-up I'd bothered to put on made a difference. Or maybe wearing civvies rather than jods made me look older. *Who knows?* The male brain was a mystery to me. It'd been years since I'd had the time—or the opportunity—for a relationship.

I nodded at the almost-full glass of lemonade in front of me. "I'm fine thanks."

"Are you sure? What about a wine?"

Resisting the temptation to roll my eyes, I shook my head. "I've some more work to do later. Need to keep a clear head."

Behind the highly polished wood of the counter, in one smooth move the Australian barman pulled a wide glass from a high shelf and angled it under the nozzle as he flicked the tap with the harp on it. Coffee-coloured beer flowed almost lazily, its creamy head growing steadily with every second.

Richard turned his dark eyes on me. "Well, this is a regular turn up for the books, seeing you up 'ere, Izzy, darlin'." He looked behind me, searching the dark corners of the bar. "Is your little friend wiv you?"

"Nope, just me."

A momentary look of disappointment crossed his face. "So, how's tricks? What brings you this far north?"

I lifted a shoulder. "Taking a couple of mares to stud. You?"

Fishing in a pocket, Muscles Mortimer pulled out a tenner, slapping it on the bar. Taking his beer from the barman, he took a long pull before setting it carefully on a beermat, then smacked his lips appreciatively. "Customers," he said succinctly. "New an' old."

My brow creased. "Old customers? I thought you were new here?"

"Well, you're a right clever one, ain't you? Can't get anythink past you." He put a hand on his chest. "I've been 'ere a few months. Enough for a couple o' shoeings. Reckon that makes me new-*ish*."

That made sense. Horses were usually shod every six weeks.

Pocketing the change the barman had counted into his hand, Richard switched the subject. "So, eh, what did 'er lady-ship say?" he asked.

I frowned again.

"When you told 'er about my visit yesterday?"

I was saved from replying by a new arrival. Craig of the amazing sea-green peepers appeared in the doorway, his black Labrador following at his heels. His eyes widened. "Izzy! Fancy seeing you here!"

Gone was his gamekeeper garb, and in its place he wore a grey down-filled gilet, charcoal jeans, ribbed t-shirt under a blue check shirt with casually pushed up sleeves, and all topped off by his blue baseball cap. Somehow he exuded effortless chic, looking more Milan than Morningside. "Craig!" I answered, stalling for time while my brain processed the sight before me. *A mystery wrapped in an enigma.*

Walking behind us, Craig leaned against the bar to my left. "Well, good evening, Izzy. Nice to see you again. Can I be getting you something?" At his feet, Jet sat down, without needing any command.

"I'm fine thanks." I looked from Craig to Richard. "Do you two know each other?"

"Aye, we've met." Craig gave the farrier a curt nod, then caught the barman's attention. "The usual thanks, Zak, when you've got a minute."

At that moment, the door swung open again. In came a heavy-set older man with eyebrows that would put a Neanderthal to shame and a handlebar moustache of the type that would usually have been accompanied by a military uniform and at least three stripes on his arm. He jerked his chin at Richard, then stomped across and sat at one of the wooden tables in the main part of the pub.

As the barman placed a bottle of beer on the counter in front of Craig, he was collared by the farrier.

"Double whisky, mate, thanks. Single malt." From his back pocket, Richard produced a roll of money and peeled off another ten pound note.

Pouring from an ornate bottle, the Ozzie dispensed some peaty-smelling amber liquid into a short, thick-bottomed glass, then handed it and some coins to Richard in exchange for the tenner.

The farrier picked up his pint and raised it in my direction. "'Scuse me, darlin'." He took the whisky in the other hand. "Gorra take this to the man." Off he went to join the sergeant major.

Craig must've seen the question on my face. "Oliver Seaforth, the local vet." He tilted his head at a table in the corner. "How about us getting a more comfy seat?"

————

"HOPE you didn't mind me crashing your conversation with Richard?" Craig said as we sat ourselves at the corner table. Jet circled twice, then lay down quietly at his feet.

"Not at all. It was hardly a conversation. He'd just started touting for business again when you arrived. You saved my bacon."

The corners of Craig's eyes crinkled. "Well, then, I'm glad to be of service." Tapping a finger on the menu cards that were propped between white porcelain salt and pepper cellars in the centre of the table, he looked at me from under the brim of his cap. "And since you were talking of bacon, I was planning to get something to eat here. Would you want to keep me company?"

I nodded. "That's why I came. Thanks, that would be nice." Then my mouth dried up. It seemed I'd lost the power of coherent speech, because the intensity of his gaze was frazzling my brain.

"Well, that's great." Craig smiled, seemingly unaware of the effect he was having on me. "Did you manage to get the mares sorted okay this afternoon?" He punctuated his question by taking a swig from his bottle of beer, which drew my attention to his lips and messed with my head even more.

Get a grip, Paterson. You're acting like a hormonal teenager. I covered my discomfort by squaring up the beermat under my drink, concentrating on getting my heart rate under control. "Yeah." I risked meeting his eyes again. "But I just about got my guts for garters from old Hamish the hard-nosed."

Craig chuckled. "Aye. Why d'you think I skedaddled out of the way before himself appeared? It's enough that I have to deal with him every morning, without meeting him in the afternoons too."

"Wait—you work with him? I thought you were a game-keeper or something. Although," I waved a hand at his outfit, "you confused me tonight." *In more ways than one.*

"I could say the same of you," he countered, pointing at my skinny jeans and open-necked white shirt. "What happened to the horsey girl look?"

I shrugged. "It's nice to get out of work clothes now and again."

"That's it, exactly." He screwed up his nose. "Those guys at the estate want me to look like I just stepped out of the pages of *Field and Stream*. It's like a uniform to them, with tweed oozing out of every orifice. But I like to rebel." He touched his cap and winked. "Just a bit."

Definitely an enigma. "You never said what you do there?"

He gave a mirthless chuckle. "They call me Pony Boy." Catching my frown, he explained further. "Actually, I'm Hamish's second-in-command at the stud. But it's me that's responsible for getting the garrons—the Highland Ponies—ready and looking after them up the hill when the shoots are on. It keeps me out of his way, too," he added with a lift of his eyebrows.

"Oh! So it's you that Hamish was talking about to the Child Catcher," I said without thinking.

"The Child Catcher?" Craig looked intrigued.

I blushed. "One of your tweed guys. Came by the stables this afternoon. Reminded me of a character in Chitty Chitty Bang Bang."

This caused a full-on laugh. "Aye, you're so right. Miles Ainsworth the gamie. Now I know where I've seen him before!"

While Craig laughed, I stared at him, a nasty suspicion brewing. *There aren't that many men that work with horses.* And many of those that did were of a certain persuasion. Especially if they did more than work with them. "So, do you ride?" I asked.

He shrugged. "Well, yes, when I can, I like to. But a lot of the time I'm leading the ponies rather than riding."

My heart sank. It was all falling into place now. Good looks. Fashionable clothes. Horse riding. *Typical!* The first attractive guy I'd met in months. *Years, actually.* And he wasn't interested in women. What was the line in that Robbie Williams song? Something about all the handsome men being gay? I stifled a sigh. *But at least he'll be good company.* I picked up a menu. "Shall we order?"

CHAPTER FIVE

My realisation that Craig wouldn't be interested in me was quite freeing. With my hormones under control, I was able to enjoy dinner—and his company—without worrying about what I said or what he'd think of me. I even relaxed enough to decide to give work a miss for the rest of the evening and treated myself to a bottle of cider. Thistly Cross, my favourite, from an East Lothian brewery not far from where I was brought up.

Around us, conversation in the pub ebbed and flowed, customers arrived and departed, meals were served and devoured—just a typical evening at a local hostelry.

Dinner long finished—a tasty mushroom risotto followed by raspberry cranachan—Craig and I had got to the part of the evening when you reminisce about TV programmes you watched as a child, arguing about who was the best character and who had the most memorable catchphrase.

We were busy discussing the Blue Peter pets—they much more important than the presenters, naturally—when the outside door opened with a gust of wind and a trim old lady stepped carefully over the threshold. Wearing a tweed skirt and cashmere jumper, she had white-grey hair permed in loose waves round her head.

For a moment I thought the Queen had come to visit.

Beside me, Craig straightened in his seat. Maybe he was thinking the same thing.

The old lady's nostrils flared as if scenting for prey, and her sharp eyes darted from left to right, scanning the room. When she spotted Craig, she hurried over. "Mr MacDonald," she said in a breathy voice, "have you seen my Hamish here this evening?"

Not the Queen, then. I was a little disappointed. It would have been a good story. And it would've been nice to know that royalty could escape protocol now and again and have a drink in a pub like the rest of us. *Poor woman.* I'd realised long ago that having lots of money wasn't all it was cracked up to be.

Craig shook his head. "I'm sorry, Mrs Douglas, he's no' been in th'night." It seemed like a few beers made Craig's accent stronger.

Hamish's wife turned her mouth down and thrust her hands onto her hips, scanning the bar again. "Where can he be?" she said, almost to herself.

"He was at the stables this afternoon," I offered. "I left him in his office."

Head tilting like a sparrow who's spotted a stray crumb, her bright eyes focussed on me. "And you are...?"

"Izzy Paterson." I held out a hand. "I work for Lady Letham. Brought a couple of mares up to stud earlier."

"Nice to meet you," she said perfunctorily, but her mind was obviously elsewhere.

"Could it be that a client brought him a bottle o' whisky, and he's in his office doing a quality check?" Craig offered, slowly spinning his empty beer bottle, rotating it on its thick base. He gave me a quick glance.

She pressed her lips together and clenched a fist. "Maybe. I'd better go check." Without a backward glance she was off, leaving the pub door swinging wildly behind her.

I raised my eyebrows at her departure, then nodded at Craig's empty bottle. "Is it my round?"

He shook his head. "I'd better call it a night. I've an early start wi' the garrons the morn." He speared me with those green eyes. "Can I walk you back to the B&B?"

My stomach flipped. "I—It's okay," I stammered, suddenly tongue-tied. Somehow, with the arrival of Mrs Douglas, the atmosphere had shifted. "There's no need. I can't imagine there's any Jack the Rippers in a wee place like this."

He lifted a shoulder. "It'll be no trouble. It's on my way home."

———

IT WAS ONLY A FEW MINUTES' walk back to the B&B, along a path beside the River Dee, which tumbled and burbled loudly enough to make conversation difficult. I buttoned my jacket against the slight nip of frost, gazing up at the canopy of stars twinkling in the velvet sky overhead. We were about twenty miles from the nearest street lights, but there was enough moonlight to easily see the path ahead.

Scattered pine needles covered the peaty earth beneath our feet, their scent mingling with wood smoke from the houses we passed and the faintest hint of Craig's signature sandalwood after-shave.

Beside me, he studied the ground as if searching for treasure, hands thrust into his pockets. Jet trotted at his heels, his nose similarly scanning the ground for secrets.

We were almost back at the guest house when I broke the silence between us. "Thanks for your company tonight, Craig.

I probably won't see you in the morning. Hamish told me to be there by ten."

The lorry—my only mode of transport up here apart from my feet—loomed out of the darkness, and Craig stopped by the cab, opposite the gate to the B&B. "Aye, my party leaves at nine." His face tightened. "You'll likely ha' left for home by the time we get off the hill."

I nodded. "Probably. Assuming Eagle does his job quickly. I can't imagine he'll have much of a bedside manner," I joked.

Craig grimaced. "No." He looked into my eyes, and my stomach did that rollercoaster thing again. "It's been good chatting wi' you the night, Izzy. It makes a change to meet a girl who's interested in more than just make-up and celebrities." He scuffed a toe on the ground. "Might you be up this way again?"

I shrugged. "Maybe. If the mares don't take and need to come see Eagle again."

"In three weeks," he said, referring to the time gap between mares' seasons. He twisted his mouth. "Or you could just come visit."

"I suppose," I said slowly, trying to work out if Lady Letham was likely to send me here again.

Obviously, I didn't sound very convincing, because his eyes darkened and he stepped closer. "Perhaps I need to persuade you." Catching my hand, he pulled me towards him. His eyes never left mine as he slowly bent his head and lightly touched his lips to mine.

I blinked in surprise. *Not gay, then.*

My brain was still processing this unexpected turn of events when his other arm circled my waist and he pulled me closer, drawing me into a kiss that was so sweet, so intense, that it had my pulse racing and every particle in my body tingling like I'd just had an electric shock.

In the distance somewhere I thought I heard sirens.

Makes a change from fireworks. Or the earth moving. His kiss really *was* that good. Reality receded again for another minute or two, while Craig's sensitive mouth ignited sparks in every fibre of my being.

When the porch light went on behind us, at first I thought it was another effect of Craig's rather talented lips— electric shocks, sirens, fireworks, and now a light show!

But then I realised that someone was maybe trying to drop a hint, and I jumped away from him, my face turning crimson. I'd told Mrs Beaton I wouldn't be out late, so she hadn't given me a key. *What will they think of me?*

He kept a hold of my hand, stopping me from fleeing. "Tell me you'll come visit again?"

I swallowed, then nodded. I didn't trust my voice.

"Or I could come down to Glengowrie next time I get a day off. If that's okay?" He handed me his phone. "Will you give me your number?"

Typing quickly, I added my number to his directory, and gave him the handset back. He pressed some buttons, and seconds later I felt my mobile buzz in my pocket.

"And now you've got mine too," he said with a smile, dropped one last butterfly kiss on my lips, then spun on his heel and walked back down the path, Jet following behind like a silent shadow.

I found my voice again. "I thought you said this was on your way?"

Turning, he walked backwards for a few steps, a big grin on his face. "I lied. I just wanted to spend some more time with you." He blew me a kiss. "Sleep well!"

CHAPTER SIX

UNSURPRISINGLY, after my emotions had been jump-started for the first time in years, I didn't sleep that well. Or at least, not that quickly.

After I left Craig, I floated along the corridor of the B&B, sure Mrs Beaton would be hovering somewhere, desperate to know who I'd been painting the village red with—me who said I'd not be out late, and had lots of work to do when I got back. *Oops.* But my luck was in, and I managed to avoid her. Perhaps my stealth-tiptoeing skills had something to do with it.

Before I finally fell asleep, I'd only replayed our kiss in my head about a hundred times. Maybe a hundred and one.

So when, minutes later—or at least, that's what it felt like —my alarm went off, it took a scalding hot shower to slough the cobwebs at least partially away. I knew it would take caffeine to get me fully awake.

With my second cup of coffee at the breakfast table, I was starting to feel more human. Fortunately for me, I wasn't the only guest in the dining room at the B&B, so Mrs Beaton hadn't yet been able to interrogate me.

I glanced across at the other table—three men in tweed, quite possibly Craig's shooting party for this morning—then checked my watch, trying to gauge how near finished they were, and whether another slice of toast would leave me alone and vulnerable to a grilling. *Probably,* I thought with a sigh, glimpsing the proprietor hovering in the background.

But I was saved by the bell—literally—a moment later when a metallic 'ding dong' echoed through the house, and Mrs Beaton scurried off down the hall. I took my chance to spread some strawberry jam on another slice of wholewheat. *I can always leave it half-eaten.* Although the waste would probably send my gran, who'd lived through the war and rationing, spinning in her grave.

What happened next would *definitely* have had my gran spinning in her grave.

I'd just sunk my teeth into the toast when Mrs B opened the door to the dining room and ushered in a policeman. "Sergeant Lovell to see you, Ms Paterson," she said, squinting at me like I was a convicted felon.

My heart stuttered. Why is it when you see a policeman you automatically feel guilty? Casting my mind back to my journey yesterday, I tried to remember if I might've been caught by any speed cameras. *Nope.* I was driving the lorry, and careful not to go above fifty, so as to give the mares a good trip. *So not speeding then.*

As he stepped into the room, I realised that this was not just *any* old policeman. No, this one was relatively young— thirties, maybe—and full-on Hollywood. *Or Pinewood at least.* He had that Jon Snow thing going on, all dark and broody. But not the shoulder-length hair. *Must be regulations. No hair trailing enticingly below your collar, PC Plod. But any amount on your face.* Would that be enough to stop coppers being mobbed in the street by Game of Thrones fans desperate for a selfie with their hero? I wasn't sure.

After what had happened last night with Craig, I couldn't believe that my hormones were in overdrive again. But this guy definitely pushed some of my buttons—the geeky medieval fantasy ones at least. Wasn't it just typical—I hadn't met a man that got my heart racing in months, probably years, and here they were like buses, two at once!

Giving myself a mental wrist-slap, I chewed manfully on the toast and tried to concentrate on what was happening around me.

The men at the other table gave the policeman sideways looks, then made a great show of pushing plates away, balling napkins, and disappearing out of the room as fast as they could without making it obvious they were hurrying.

Mrs Beaton took her time gathering the plates off their table, no doubt so she could eavesdrop on what the policeman was there for. But she could only spin it out so long, before she had to clear things to the kitchen where presumably she'd have her ear to the door.

I rolled my eyes, then blushed as Detective Night's Watch appeared in front of me and nodded at the seat opposite.

"If it wouldn't be too much trouble, may I join you, Ms Paterson?"

Drat. He must've thought my eye roll was to do with him. I nodded, trying frantically to swallow toast which had turned to cardboard in my mouth. "How can I help you?" I spluttered, spraying toast crumbs everywhere. *Nice one, Izzy. Jon Snow won't forget you now—he'll have to dry-clean his uniform because of you.*

Pulling a notebook and stubby pencil out of one of the many pockets adorning his jacket, Sergeant Lovely, *sorry, Lovell,* looked across at me from under his dark eyebrows. "I just need you to confirm your whereabouts yesterday afternoon, Ms Paterson." His voice was like melted chocolate, but sadly didn't have that Winterfell northern accent.

Maybe just as well. It wouldn't do to have my brain turn to mush when I was being interrogated by the fuzz. I took a calming breath. "I drove up from Glengowrie to deliver some mares to the stud at Balmoral. Then I came here." I nodded at the dining room door. This time I managed not to douse him in carbohydrate flecks.

He wrote something in his notebook, then looked at me for a moment, his head cocked and his lips pressed together. "Ms Paterson, I'm afraid I'll need to ask you to come down to the station and make a witness statement."

I frowned. "Now? I need to check on the mares. What's all this about? Taking a couple of mares to stud isn't usually something that would interest the police."

He gave me a level gaze. "Just an incident at the castle, miss. We're talking to everyone who was on the estate yesterday afternoon and evening." His forehead creasing, he scribbled a few more words in his notebook.

Perhaps I shouldn't have questioned him. Did that make me look guilty? *But you haven't done anything, Izzy. Get a grip.* And maybe *not* questioning him would have made me look *more* guilty. Who knew? Obviously not me—I totally wasn't cut out to be a criminal. *But... maybe I didn't imagine the sirens last night after all?* My face coloured at the memory.

My rambling thoughts were interrupted by Sergeant Sexy, who stood up and pocketed his notebook, narrowing his eyes when he spotted my pink cheeks. "Now would be perfect, Miss Paterson. The estate is out of bounds this morning, anyway; things are cordoned off till this afternoon for the investigation." Anticipating my next question, he added, "but the horses are all fine and we've a vet in attendance just in case."

———

MAYBE I'VE WATCHED TOO many cop shows on TV, but, sitting in that little room with the tape recorder and the CCTV camera and Detective Dark and Handsome sat opposite me, it was hard not to feel guilty. *At least he let me drive the lorry here.* I'd have totally felt like a felon in the back of a police car.

The introductions done and recorded, the sergeant gave me a smile. "Nothing to worry about, Miss Paterson. We just need your witness statement to establish some of the facts about yesterday." He glanced down at his notebook. "Firstly, can you tell me the purpose of your visit here, and when you arrived?" He might have made it sound like a formality, but he still watched me carefully from under those heavy brows.

Trying to be succinct, I explained about taking the mares to stud. "I arrived at the stud about four o'clock I think and left again probably quarter to five. Then I went to the B&B."

"Is there anyone who could confirm those timings?"

"Well, Mrs Beaton I guess. Hamish and Stan at the stables. Hamish Douglas. I forget Stan's surname."

He wrote in his notebook. "Anybody else?"

"Craig. Craig MacDonald. He directed me to the stables—"

"So it was your first time there?" Sergeant Lovell interrupted.

No flies on him. "Yeah. I've only been up here—in Glengowrie—three weeks."

His chin tilted. "And where were you before?"

"London. I worked for BleuBank."

This gave him pause. "And now you're working with horses?" You could almost see his brain trying to process the disjoint.

"Yeah. It was my hobby before. But I got myself qualified as a horse trainer so I could change career. Although," *guess I should tell him in case he already knows,* "I still do some consulting on a part-time basis."

"Consulting?" His eyebrows asked the question.

"IT investigations. Computer security."

"Oh-kay." His brow quirked briefly, then his pencil flew over the page some more. "Returning to your visit to the stud. Once you got there, did you see anyone else who could confirm the timings?"

"There was some man visited while I was there. The gamekeeper I think. Tall, thin man, talking to Hamish about a shoot tomorrow. Today, I mean," I corrected myself. "They were going out at nine o'clock." Reflexively, I checked my watch. Five past nine. *Good.* I wasn't late for Hamish. *Can't imagine that would go down well.* Although, since the estate was out of bounds, our appointment was probably off. *Poor Allegra and Daisy.* I'd need to get a number and try to phone him.

"And after you got to the Beatons?"

"I did some work, then went out to The Queen's Arms for something to eat."

"What time was that?"

I puffed out a breath, raising my eyes to the ceiling as I tried to remember. "Just before seven, I think."

"And when did you arrive back at the B&B?"

My mind flipped to the pub. And Craig. And the kiss. My cheeks flushed. "About ten fifteen."

Detective Eagle Eyes must've noticed my pink cheeks. A dark eyebrow raised just a millimetre. "And can anyone confirm those timings?"

"I think Mrs Beaton heard me come back. She put the porch light on. At the pub there was the barman who served me when I arrived. An Ozzie guy called Zak. Richard Mortimer the farrier arrived just after me. He spoke to me briefly and then was chatting for a while with another man I didn't recognise, an older, chunky guy with a handlebar moustache. I was told he was a vet. A few locals were there too—Craig MacDonald was one of them." I refrained from mentioning that I'd ended up spending the evening with him. "And Mrs Douglas came in quite late, maybe about ten. Oh!" I clamped my hand to my mouth. "She was looking for Hamish." Dread filled my stomach. "Is everything okay?"

———

BEFORE PC PERFECT had a chance to answer—although no doubt I'd have got a non-answer—there was a knock at the door.

A fair-haired policewoman peeked round the door jamb. "Sarge, the initial PM report came back. You need to see this." She nodded over her shoulder into the corridor.

With a grimace, Sergeant Lovell shuffled his papers together and stood up. "Excuse me a moment. I'll not be long."

PM. *Post Mortem*. All the blood drained from my face. *Someone is dead.* Someone at the castle, from what he'd said about the estate being cordoned off. And Hamish had been missing last night. Could it be him? *That could explain why they're questioning me.* I remembered the dagger-like letter opener on his desk. *Could someone have stabbed him in his office?*

That thought stilled me for a moment, sympathy for Mrs Douglas washing over me. She'd seemed genuinely worried about Hamish last night, so she'd presumably be devastated if he'd been killed.

I glanced at the CCTV camera in the corner. *I hope they don't think I'm a suspect.* But what was it they said on all the cop shows? Means, motive, and opportunity, wasn't it?

If thinking he was a misogynistic git counts as motive, I'm sunk. But how would I have done it? *Knifed him with my rapier-sharp wit?* I bit back a smile. But I couldn't deny I'd been there yesterday. So if Hamish was indeed dead, and if foul play was involved, then I'd surely be a suspect, since I had 'opportunity'.

My heart sank further. *Should I be asking them to get me a lawyer?*

———

THREE QUARTERS OF AN HOUR LATER, after giving a DNA sample "purely to rule you out of our investigations" and having my fingerprints taken, I was finally allowed to go.

Sergeant Lovell escorted me along the cream-painted corridor from the interview room. "Please stay where we can get in touch with you, Ms Paterson," he said, swiping his warrant card through a device beside the door leading to the foyer. "I'll not ask for your passport." The side of his mouth twitched, the first sign of humanity I'd seen from him. "But please, don't leave the country or I'll be getting demoted to traffic duty."

I gave him a mock salute. "Don't worry. It's hard to even get a day off when you've got horses to look after."

His hand paused on the door handle. "So you get a day off?"

"Sundays. In theory. If there's not a show to attend, or a sick horse to nurse or some other emergency. So maybe if there's a pig flying or a blue moon." I shrugged. "I still need to do my horses. No rest for the wicked." *Oops. Bad choice of words in a police station, Izzy.*

Warm brown eyes stared into mine as he held the door open. "What about the evenings? Surely you don't work *all* the time? European Work Directive and all that."

"Yeah, I usually get evenings off. Although half the time I'm comatose on the couch." With a wry grin, I indicated my less-than athletic body. "I'm still getting used to all the hard work."

He waved me through the opening. "I'm sure it gets easier." For the first time, I saw him smile, and it was like the sun came out at Winterfell. Almost as an afterthought, he handed me a business card. "Call me if you remember anything else." His chin jerked up in farewell. "Be careful out there."

———

"GOOD MORNING, IZZY," a voice greeted me as I stepped into the foyer of the police station.

I startled, my eyes widening as I recognised Craig sitting there in the shadows, wearing his tweed and tattersall work gear, with blue smudges under his eyes. *Probably my fault for keeping him up late.*

"Oh, hi," I said lamely, sure my cheeks were turning pink.

He inclined his head at the door behind me and raised his eyebrows. "I think you've got an admirer."

With a jerk of my head, I glanced quickly over my shoulder. Sergeant Lovell was disappearing down the corridor. "Him?" I said incredulously. "No way."

Craig lifted a shoulder.

I blinked at him for a moment, then decided it would be politic to change the subject. "What brings you here? I thought you were off on a shoot this morning." Even as I said it, I realised the answer. The sergeant had said they were speaking to everyone who was on the estate yesterday afternoon.

"The shoot got cancelled. They've got me here for questioning." His lips pressed together. "Voluntarily. At the moment." Glancing across at the desk sergeant, who was squinting at something on a computer monitor, Craig's shoulders slumped. "But if I'm honest, I'm not sure if that'll last—I'm their number one suspect."

The breath left my lungs. "What? Suspect? What for? And why on earth would they think that?"

Craig opened a palm. "I'm Hamish's assistant. So with him gone..." he trailed off, swiping his hat off his head and running long fingers through his curly hair. "They think I was after wanting his job."

Ice trickled down my spine. "So... Hamish died?"

"Aye, I'm afraid so. He was kicked in the head by a horse." Worry made him look like a little boy caught stealing apples, and my heart twisted.

So I was right about it being Hamish. But not about the dagger. "But why would they blame you for that? Anyone could get kicked."

Hands balling the cap in his lap, he nodded. "Aye. But they came back not half an hour ago, adamant that they needed to ask me more questions."

Frowning, I protested, "But isn't it usually the wife that does it?" Behind me, a door snicked open. "In all the cop shows, anyway. Although Mrs Douglas didn't strike me—"

I was interrupted by a throat clearing pointedly.

The cute constable. *Great.*

"We're ready for you now, Mr MacDonald." Sergeant Lovell's brown eyes were no longer warm.

With a sigh of resignation, Craig got to his feet. "I'll see you later," he said as he passed me, then flicked me a worried glance. "Hopefully."

CHAPTER SEVEN

THE LOOK on Craig's face as he got taken off for questioning stayed with me all the way back to the B&B. He looked stricken, and it pierced me to my soul. Although I didn't know him very well, I couldn't believe someone as nice as him would have committed a crime.

But it seemed like the police didn't think Hamish's death was just an accident after all. *That must be why they took my DNA and fingerprints.* It *should* rule me out, but they were obviously suspicious of Craig as well, and, because of his job, Craig's DNA and fingerprints would be in a lot of the same places that Hamish would frequent.

I hated the feeling of being in the frame for a possible murder. And I'd bet Craig didn't like that feeling either. But if it wasn't either of us, then who was it? *And why?* Driving on autopilot, I churned over the few things I knew.

One: Hamish was dead. Two: He'd been kicked by a horse, but the police appeared to think it was suspicious. Three: That meant it probably happened at the stables, or perhaps in the fields nearby. Four: It must've happened some time between me leaving his office yesterday afternoon and whenever I heard the sirens last evening. *Or maybe earlier, since Mrs Douglas was looking for him at the pub.* And surely he'd have gone home for dinner after work? So that would leave only a couple of hours in the evening. But wouldn't he be at home then, rather than the stables? It was very strange.

I tapped a finger on the steering wheel, mulling it over. *Means, motive, opportunity.*

A lot of people would probably have had the opportunity —the estate was so big it must have plenty of staff. But *why* would someone want to kill the stud manager?

Yes, *I* had opportunity. But I had no reason to kill Hamish. Craig might have had a motive, but he was with me in the pub all evening...

Compulsive sweeper Stan should probably also be in the frame, but one fleeting resentful glance wasn't enough to build a case on. And was annoyance enough of a reason to want your boss dead? *Surely not.*

The child catcher gamekeeper had also been around in the afternoon, but he'd been and gone really quickly. And again, what would be his motive?

My circuitous thoughts came back to Mrs Douglas. Would she have had grounds to kill her husband? Was he as bigoted towards her as he'd been to me? But then, why stay married? She could surely have divorced him years ago if there'd been any issues.

Pulling the lorry to a stop outside the guest house, I sighed. Without more facts to go on, I was getting nowhere. But if there was anything I could do to stop Craig or me getting charged with murder, I had to do it.

I sat taller, flexed my fingers, and smiled grimly. *Perhaps this is a situation where I can put my non-horsey talents to good use.* I glanced across at the B&B. But first I'd have to stonewall Mrs B's inevitable questions and gather my stuff so I was ready to go home.

———

IT TURNED out that "I've been instructed by the police not to divulge any information" was enough to keep the guest house owner from questioning me too closely—for a while at least.

Instead, she took particular delight in telling me in great detail about how the police had been asking about my whereabouts yesterday, and how she 'just had' to tell them she'd seen me outside last night with a 'young man'.

Rats. I'd glossed over that with Sergeant Lovell, omitting to tell him that Craig had walked me home. But I probably should've mentioned it. *Craig might need it for an alibi.* Sliding my hand into my pocket to check I hadn't lost the policeman's card, I resolved to phone him soon.

In the meantime I needed to extricate myself from Mrs Beaton's hallway and pack, and then I had to text Trinity with an update. After that I had some research to do, before the stables re-opened in the afternoon and I could go check on the mares.

When Mrs B next paused for breath, I checked my watch theatrically. "Oh! You'll have to excuse me." Before she could start talking again, I hurried off down the corridor. "I really should get packed so I can get away back to Glengowrie," I threw over my shoulder.

Reaching the sanctuary of the lace-bedecked boudoir, I closed the bedroom door behind me and leaned back against the white-painted panels. My eyes closed, I let out a long breath, feeling guilty for not being more friendly.

Maybe I should've stayed to gossip. I might've found out more about Hamish. But I found intense people like Mrs Beaton very draining, and it had been a difficult morning already. I picked up my bag and started to throw my stuff into it. *Some things are just a bit beyond the call of duty.*

———

ONCE I WAS SAFELY BACK out in the lorry, I drove along to The Queen's Arms and parked outside. They were open to serve coffees, and there was an hour or so before I could get into the estate, so I could top up my caffeine levels and do some research at the same time. *Result!*

The pub in daytime was a revelation. It smelled of furniture polish and the varnished wood surfaces were gleaming. Somehow it was brighter inside too, and, even though it was still morning, they had the log fire blazing in the grate, making everything seem quite cheery.

Behind the bar this time was a stick-thin Polish girl in her twenties, dyed blonde hair scraped back into a pony tail, black clothing making her pale skin look almost grey. While she was making my drink, I seated myself in a booth near to the fire and logged in to the wi-fi.

After half an hour's internet sleuthing and a large cappuccino, I'd uncovered some information about Hamish which made me see him in a different light.

With most people, I could find out quite a lot merely by checking out their social media profiles—who they were friends with, events they attended, photos they appeared in. But the stud manager, perhaps unsurprisingly, didn't appear to 'do' social media.

However, a Google search *did* spit out something interesting.

Like I'd thought when I was in his ultra-tidy office, Hamish was ex-military.

In the eighties, as a member of the Household Cavalry, he'd bravely leapt to the Queen's rescue when a lone gunman fired shots at her during the Trooping the Colour parade in London. His courageous actions had probably saved the sovereign from a nasty end. *I guess his reward was a job for life here at the stud.*

A wave of sadness washed over me. If he'd been a trooper in the Household Cavalry, he'd have been a great rider in his prime, and a good horseman. It was a shame the world had lost such knowledge and experience.

But Hamish's quick thinking back in 1981 had thwarted the ambitions of Marcus Sarjeant, a seventeen-year-old who'd been desperate for the fame and notoriety he'd gain by attacking the Queen. Later that year Marcus had been convicted of treason, then served three years in a psychiatric prison.

The thing that caught my attention was that, on release, the wannabe assassin had changed his name and disappeared into obscurity.

Doing some mental arithmetic, I worked out that Marcus would be in his 50s now. Could he have tracked Hamish down all these years later and wreaked his revenge? *Possibly.*

Would he really have waited that long, though? *Probably not.*

I sat back in my chair and drummed my fingers on the armrest, staring out of the window, eyes fixed on the dark green fronds of the pine trees opposite, but not really seeing them.

The Trooping the Colour attack was definitely a lead, and something to follow-up on. But logic surely implied that it would be something more recent that had inspired the ex-cavalryman's murder? I needed to dig deeper about Hamish and his work here at Balmoral, to see if I could tease out any motives for murder.

Time for the heavy guns.

Flexing my fingers, I fired up Gremlin, the app I'd written specifically for burrowing into the deep web, and set it to hunting for additional information about the stud manager.

CHAPTER EIGHT

Wʜɪʟᴇ Gʀᴇᴍʟɪɴ ᴡᴏʀᴋᴇᴅ ɪᴛs ᴍᴀɢɪᴄ, I took out my phone and texted Trinity, updating her on what had happened, though I didn't tell her about last night's dinner. And afterwards. That would take longer than a text message.

Next, I dialled the number on Sergeant Lovell's card.

Perhaps unsurprisingly, since he was probably still interrogating Craig, I got his answering service. *Grrr.* "It's Izzy Paterson," I enunciated carefully. "I have some more information for you if you could phone me back please?" With a sigh of relief, I ended the call. *I hate these things.*

In fact, I avoided speaking on phones wherever possible, preferring email or text messages. At least that way the person could read your message when they got time, and their reply wouldn't interrupt anything important. A little voice told me that I was probably just projecting—I had an aversion to phone calls because I somehow always managed to get tongue-tied or embarrass myself.

Gremlin hadn't produced any results yet, but it was after noon, so time to try a trip over to the estate to check on the mares. Pausing the app, I packed up and made my way back out to the lorry.

Of course, inevitably, Sergeant Lovell called back when I was driving to the stables, and there was no hands-free connection in the lorry. By the time I'd found somewhere on the narrow road to pull over and speak safely, he'd rung off. Growling with frustration, I hit 'redial' and finally got through to him.

The sound of that chocolatey voice soothed my irritation somewhat. "Ms Paterson! I didn't expect to hear from you so soon."

"Yes, well..." I rubbed my forehead. *How do I broach this?* "It's just... There was something else about last night I forgot to tell you. I—uh—Craig MacDonald walked me back to the B&B. Just to make sure I found it in the dark," I added hurriedly. "So he can corroborate on the time I left the pub."

There was a brief silence on the other end of the line. *Probably scribbling in that notebook of his.* "And obviously that means you can account for Mr MacDonald's whereabouts at that time too."

"Yeah, I guess so. Plus I think Mrs Beaton saw us arrive back, as I said earlier."

"And would anyone be able to vouch for what time you left The Queen's Arms?"

I pressed my lips together. "Maybe the barman, I'm not sure. Richard Mortimer and the man he was speaking to had gone by then. But we left just after Mrs Douglas asked us about Hamish, about ten o'clock I think."

Another silence. *More scribbling, no doubt.* "Okay, thank you Ms Paterson. Feel free to call me again if you've forgotten to tell me anything else."

I could almost hear the air quotes around the word 'forgotten', and my cheeks pinked, despite the fact that he couldn't see me. "Of course," I replied, suitably chastised.

FIFTEEN MINUTES later I'd negotiated my way through security and into the estate, and had parked the lorry in the parking area in front of the outdoor school.

There was a police car parked outside the closest cottage, sides chequered in blue and yellow, light bar strapped across its roof. A uniformed policewoman stood guard at the entrance to the stable yard, thumbs hooked in the edges of her flak vest, blue and white police tape fluttering in the breeze behind her.

At least with the police here, the murderer should keep well away. That thought gave me pause. *Maybe you should've thought of that before you returned to the scene of a crime, Izzy?* I rolled my eyes at my own stupidity and briefly considered cranking up the engine again and hot-footing it back home.

Then my shoulders relaxed. *But surely the police must think it's safe, or they'd not have opened the estate up again.* So maybe not so stupid after all. And I *did* have the mares to look after.

Across to my right, two paddocks away, I spotted the girls, heads down and happily munching on lush green grass.

Pulling a couple of grooming brushes from a box in the opposite footwell and a Puffa jacket from behind the seat, I stepped out of the lorry and shrugged on the extra layer.

Today's weather was less typical for May, but more typical for the Highlands—oppressive grey clouds obscured most of the sky, and the wind held a hint of winter cold rather than summer warmth.

I shivered. *Still haven't got used to this Scottish weather.* It was at least two degrees colder up here than it was in London, but on days like this it felt like the Arctic, not the Highlands. Especially when I'd just been sitting in front of a roaring log fire in the pub.

Under the clock tower, the policewoman had stiffened,

presumably a response to my arrival rather than the cold. Narrowing my eyes, I stuffed the brushes into my pockets. Then I walked round the front of the lorry to retrieve the mares' passports from the glove box on the passenger side, in case she got all officious on me.

"Afternoon, Ms Paterson," said a male voice behind me.

I just about jumped out of my skin, banged my elbow on the lorry door and managed to drop the passports at the same time.

"Forgive me!" Sergeant Lovell bent quickly to retrieve the booklets and held them out to me. "I didn't mean to give you a fright. Are you okay?"

One hand hanging onto the lorry door to keep me upright, I had the other on my chest, waiting for my heart to stop pounding. "I wasn't expecting to see you here."

He gestured at the cottage behind him. "Needed to speak to Mrs Douglas."

"Ah."

Mocha-coloured eyes regarded me in silence. Was there a hint of a smile on those full lips?

It was when his head tilted questioningly that I realised I'd been staring at his mouth, and that he was expecting me to speak. "I—uh, came to check on the mares." I pulled one of the brushes out of my pocket as evidence, hoping my cheeks hadn't gone pink and betrayed where my thoughts had been headed. "They're just over there." I pointed at the paddock.

The sergeant's jaw clamped, and he glanced across at the policewoman by the entrance, then back at me. "Check in with PC Adamson first, then. Tell her I said it was okay." Touching the side of his uniform cap like a mini salute, his brown eyes burned into mine. "Till next time," he said, then spun on his heel and strode back to his squad car.

For a moment, I watched his retreating back, my stomach

churning. Why did he affect me so? I liked Craig, didn't I? With a shake of my head, I took a deep breath, then walked across to where the constable was stationed. "Afternoon," I greeted her.

"Ma'am." She bobbed her head, giving me the once-over from under the brim of her hat. In the flattering black of her police garb, she had the look of someone who went to the gym regularly, and her glossy, raven-coloured hair and matching fingernails made me think she was also familiar with the insides of a beauty salon.

I pointed at the mares. "Sergeant Lovell said it would be okay for me to go over and check on my horses? I think I can get through the field gate over there, or I'll climb the fence."

She frowned at me and quirked a perfectly arched eyebrow. "Got some documentation to prove they're yours?"

Opening the passports at the pages that described the horses, I nodded across at the mares and handed her the booklets. "Allegra is the bay—brown with black legs—her full name is Glengowrie Allegretto. The white one—grey, in horsey parlance—is Glengowrie Miss Contrary. We call her Daisy."

Constable Jobsworth's mouth pursed as she perused the paperwork, lips showing tell-tale vertical lines that made me wonder if she was a smoker. But she smelled of some rather overpowering perfume rather than cigarettes. So perhaps not.

She spent a full minute flicking through the pages suspiciously, but seemed unable to find anything untoward, so with a slight shake of her head she closed the booklets and slipped them into their sleeve. "They seem to be in order, Miss—?" She paused expectantly, holding the passports out to me.

"Paterson. Isobel Paterson. I work for Lady Letham who owns the mares."

Her head jerked back, and I got a sharp look that wouldn't have been out of place from a magpie. "You were interviewed by the sergeant earlier." A statement, not a question.

I nodded. "Yeah, the mares arrived yesterday afternoon, and he said they were speaking to everyone who'd been on the estate that day."

A muscle tightened in her jaw and her nostrils flared slightly as she looked me up and down again.

What's her problem? I held up one of the brushes. "I just want to check on the girls and give them a groom. I won't be long."

Her face didn't lose the mistrustful look, but she jerked her chin at the horses. "On you go then," she said grudgingly. "But stay where I can see you."

With a mumbled, "Thanks," *for nothing,* I hurried off and let myself in through the five-bar gate in the paddock to the right of the road in front of the stables, and made my way across to the next enclosure, where I unbuckled the mares' head collars from the gate. When I approached, Allegra's head came up, and she snorted in alarm, making Daisy stop eating and stare at me suspiciously.

"It's only me, silly," I crooned, sending out calming vibes and angling my shoulders so they weren't directly facing the mares, to seem less aggressive. Allegra's neck relaxed, and Daisy took a step towards me. "Want a treat?" I asked, fishing in my pocket for a polo mint.

It was there that Craig found me ten minutes later, grooming the grey while the bay hung out nearby, hopeful that another sweetie would be forthcoming. Allegra noticed him first, her suddenly alert pose warning me that someone was coming.

When I saw who it was, my heart skipped a beat. "Craig! Glad to see they let you go."

He pressed his lips together. "And so am I." Taking a step closer, he scratched Allegra's shoulder, getting her instantly onside. Outwardly she seemed like a suspicious creature, but in reality she was a softie. *Bit like me.* "But they've told me I'm not allowed to go anywhere."

"Yeah, I got the same warning." Stopping grooming, I let out a long breath. "It's hard to believe that the guy who was all red-faced and grumpy yesterday afternoon is... gone." I looked across at him. "Must be worse for you, since you worked with him."

"Aye, I havenae got my head round it yet. The man's been here, like, forever. Long before I started. And," he shoved a stray curl back under the brim of his cap and re-seated it on his head, "it's such a strange way for him to go. I mean, getting kicked like that."

Shaking his head, he moved his arm in an arc to indicate the surrounding fields. "All the horses we have here are quiet as mice." His mouth turned down at the corners. "The queen's in her nineties. She's no' a spring chicken any more. So we darenae have anything difficult or dangerous around her."

I frowned. "Did you hear which horse it was?" Then my eyes widened as a terrible thought struck me. "It wasn't one of these two, was it?"

"I don't think so." He pointed a finger at the stable yard. "If you look, all the police tape is at the stables. So I suppose it must've happened there."

"Makes sense. What horses use the stables? Eagle was in when I was there yesterday."

"Aye, and the other stallions. And the mares who're close to foaling come in from the fields at night. And any garrons who're getting used up the hill the next day."

I sucked air through my teeth. "That doesn't narrow it down much."

"No, it doesnae." Fishing in his pocket, Craig found a piece of carrot and offered it to Allegra. The mare did her magician's assistant thing and disappeared it in a trice. "But I suppose we'll be finding out in due course."

"You'll have a friend for life there," I said, changing the subject and tilting my head at the bay. "That's Allegra. This one is Daisy."

He grinned and caught my eye. "I like me a nice brunette."

My heart skipped a beat again. *Is he flirting with me?* I was totally out of practice if he was. "I prefer a chestnut myself," I said, glancing at his ginger hair to check it hadn't magically changed colour in the trip from the police station to the estate. "As long as it hasn't got white socks." That was a reference only a horseman would get—chestnut horses have a reputation for being difficult, particularly if they're mares, and even more so if they have white legs.

Suppressing a smile, Craig reached down theatrically and pulled his trouser leg up an inch. "Black," he said, angling his ankle so I could see it.

"Good choice." I nodded approvingly. "But that makes you more of a bay, doesn't it?"

"Bright bay, maybe?"

"Still not a chestnut," I said playfully.

He rolled his eyes. "I'll wear the red socks tomorrow, just for you."

I grimaced. "I may not be here to see it. Or I shouldn't. But—" I rubbed Daisy's face, "I guess it depends whether we've introduced the girls to Eagle. Or not. Hamish said he and Stan would have Eagle service them today..." I trailed off.

Craig's gaze drifted across to the stables, his expression turning serious. "Well, I suppose that would be up to me, now," he said, then scratched his chin while he eyed up the two mares. "Are they shod behind?"

"No. Daisy is barefoot; Allegra just has shoes in front."

Pulling his cap off his head, he ran a hand though his

curls. "So they cannae kick chunks out of a stallion, even if he's being really annoying." His gaze fell on the paddock beside them, which was empty. "D'you know, I'm a great believer in keeping things simple. Hows about we move Eagle so he's next door, and they can be getting to know each other over the fence." He patted Allegra's neck, then gave me a sideways look. "And after that, if all goes well, we can put them together and let nature take its course."

"That sounds like a plan." And it meant I didn't have to deal with Stan the creepy stud groom again.

"D'you think Lady Letham would be okay with leaving them here for a few weeks? That way we'll be knowing they've definitely been covered." One eyebrow quirked up. "And maybe I could meet you for a drink at the pub again, when you come back to collect the mares?" Frown lines appeared on his forehead. "Unless you're seeing thon policeman?"

Taken aback, I made a face. "No, why would you think that?"

Both eyebrows quirked up this time. "Because he's got the hots for you."

I raised my eyes heavenwards. "It's like being back at primary school!" But I couldn't stop a tiny grin creeping over my face. *Craig wants to see me again.* "Want me to help you shift Eagle?" Scanning the fields around us, I spotted him in one of the paddocks closer to the stables.

"If you want to. It's up to you," Craig replied in a way that totally meant 'yes'.

I unbuckled Daisy's head collar and held it up. "We could use this to move him?"

"Aye, good idea. He's usually quiet enough." With a sideways glance at the policewoman standing guard at the stables, he added, "And I don't think they'll be allowing us on the yard yet, so we wouldnae be able to collect one, anyway."

———

EAGLE SPOTTED us coming and had trotted down to the gate before we'd even got it open. But something about him was a little off, compared to his demeanour when I'd seen him yesterday. There were lines round his eyes almost like he was worried about something, and his mouth seemed pinched. Quite different to the proud, happy horse I'd seen yesterday.

"Does he seem okay to you?" I asked.

Craig looked up from fastening the head collar on. "Say again?"

I pointed at the stallion. "He looks—" I wrinkled my nose, "upset, maybe? D'you think he somehow knows about Hamish?"

Frowning, Craig rubbed the stallion's forehead, his eyes giving the horse a quick once-over. "Looks okay to me." He handed me the lead rope. "Would you hold him a minute, and I'll just check his legs."

While Craig ran his hands down each leg in turn, I took the chance to reach out to the stallion with some calming vibes. Closing my eyes to intensify the feelings, I laid a hand on his neck.

Almost immediately, a wall of emotions assailed me—fear, worry, anger. I'd hardly managed to process this, when a picture sprang into my mind. It was in black and white, and dimly lit as if it was night, but I could see the dark, bulky shape of a man in front of me, and, down at my feet, something long, thin and sinuous. Fear overwhelmed me again, and the vision disappeared.

I opened my eyes, reeling on my feet, and would've fallen over if Craig hadn't caught me by the arm.

"Are you okay?" Concern flared in his green eyes.

"Not sure," I said, leaning my hands on my knees and shaking my head to clear it. *What just happened?*

Craig frowned. "Izzy, did you eat anything today?"

"Uh—" I pursed my lips while I thought about it. "Breakfast at the B&B. Coffee later."

He took my elbow. "Once we get Eagle moved, I'll take you to the visitor café at the castle. I think we need to get some food in you."

Five minutes later, Eagle had arrived at his new digs, and was trotting up and down the fence line, neck arched and tail in the air, showing off to the ladies next door. There was no sign of the... *whatever it was* I'd felt from him earlier.

I shook my head. Maybe I'd imagined it. *Lack of food. You were seeing things.* That must be it.

Allegra and Daisy had decided that checking out the stallion was much more entertaining than eating grass, and they stood together at the other side of the fence, goggle-eyed. You could almost see them nudging each other and saying, *'Ooh, he's not bad, is he?'*

"They'll soon be settling down." There were crinkles at the corners of Craig's eyes as he stood watching the horses, a sign of a true horse-lover. My heart warmed to him a little more. "D'you want to come back here later and we'll put them in together?"

"Okay." I checked my watch. "But I'll really need to get going after that. I've left Trinity on her own for too long. It's not fair on her."

He nodded. "Of course. But let's go and get you some food in you now."

CHAPTER NINE

A SHORT TIME LATER, I was seated in the crowded visitors' café behind Balmoral Castle. A bright room with large picture windows along one wall, there was outside seating we might've used in better weather, but the grey clouds were threatening rain.

Inside the café, there were plastic tartan tablecloths, white rail-back chairs, white-painted woodwork and a polished wood floor which gave an ambience somewhere between a simple Shaker dining room and tourist kitsch.

Craig had made me sit down while he went and got the food, so that gave me a few minutes alone.

Of course, my thoughts immediately went to what had happened in Eagle's field. Perhaps I *had* been seeing things, but... I stared down at the table, picking abstractedly at the edge of the table mat.

Hadn't I been getting better, lately, at tuning in to horses' body language and emotions? And didn't that mean that sometimes I could superimpose my feelings—usually calming vibes—to affect their mood? So was it so implausible that Eagle could somehow reflect *his* feelings back to me?

Tapping a finger on the table top, I replayed the scene in my head, and realised that it had only been when I *touched* him that I'd made that connection with the stallion. But had that—dream, vision, whatever it was—had it come from Eagle too? *And does that mean he was there when Hamish died?* That would certainly explain his mood. But what did the picture he'd projected to me *mean*?

"Penny for them?" Craig arrived back carrying a laden tray and sat down opposite me. Placing a bowl of soup, cutlery and a chunk of crusty bread in front of me, he unloaded his own coffee, then propped the empty tray against the table leg.

"Oh, nothing, just..." I took a mouthful of the soup. "This is nice." I smacked my lips appreciatively. "What is it?"

"It's the sweet potato and leek," he answered, then made a circling motion with his finger. "Just... what?"

I spread some butter on the bread. "Just," my forehead creased, "d'you think maybe it was Eagle that kicked Hamish? Might that explain the funny mood he was in earlier?"

Craig blew on the top of his Americano before taking a sip. "That could be it, I suppose. He was on our list, wasn't he?"

"Yeah." I chewed on the bread. "Poor boy, if it was him."

"Aye." He winked at me. "But maybe your mares will improve his mood."

That made me laugh. "True."

"Are you feeling any better now?"

Giving him a quick smile, I nodded. "Yeah, this is good. Just what I needed. Thanks."

"Good." His face softened. "The food is all home-made here. Not the cheapest—" he twisted his mouth wryly, "—there's a bit of a captive market here with all the tourists. But it's good food."

"So why are you not eating?"

"I had a sandwich at the cottage earlier, after I got back from the police station."

"Okay." I looked down at my soup, then back up at him. "If I'd been as organised as that, then maybe I wouldn't have nearly fainted all over you."

He quirked an eyebrow. "That might be so. But then I wouldn't have had this chance to enjoy your company and top up my caffeine levels."

That made me smile. "You can't be as much of a caffeine addict as me. I almost need intravenous coffee to get my brain in gear in the mornings."

"You're a woman after my own heart!" he laughed, lifting his cup in salute.

In the brief silence that followed while he sipped his coffee and I slurped my soup, Eagle's vision popped back into my head. I found myself wondering again about the man shape I'd seen. Initially I'd thought it was Hamish himself, but now I wondered. Hamish had been small and wiry, but the shadowy shape in the picture Eagle had shown me was taller and wider, which probably ruled out creepy Stan too.

"Craig—do you really think Hamish was killed by accident? Or might someone have done it deliberately and made it look like a horse did it?"

"Well... possibly." Craig didn't look convinced.

"But you know—knew—him better than I do. Is there anyone here on the estate who had a reason to be angry at him?"

Letting out a mirthless laugh, Craig put his cup down. "That man! He had few friends, I'm sorry to say," he said, rolling his eyes. "So just about anyone at Balmoral could have a beef with him."

I grimaced. "That doesn't narrow things down much. But why kill him *now*? Did something happen these last few days?"

Craig's eyes looked up and to the left as if he was replaying scenes in his imagination. Then his head moved slowly from side to side. "No, not that I know of."

My shoulders sagged. "It's just, if it was deliberate, I think we'll both be suspects. And I'd like to get us off the hook. So if we could work out who might have done it, we can pass it on to the police."

Running a hand through his hair, Craig blew out a breath. "It would certainly be good not to be a suspect. It has me feeling like I need to look over my shoulder the whole time."

"Mmm. Tell me about it."

"But *how* would we work out who did it? We don't even know for sure which horse it was that kicked him—or where, for that matter. Or even exactly when. The police are keeping it close to their chests. Should we not just be leaving them to do their job?"

"We could. But that still leaves us as suspects." Stalling, I took a sip of my soup, then set the spoon down and leaned my elbow on the table. "The thing is... You know I said last night that I did some computer work on the side? Well, one of the things I do is internet investigations. So I did some searches on Hamish this morning and found out he used to be in the military. He once foiled an attack on the Queen, and I wondered if that might've been a reason he got killed."

Craig's eyes widened. "Is that right? How long ago was it? He's been here at the estate for years."

"Yeah, that's where my theory falls down. It was 1981, and the attacker got out of prison in eighty-four, then disappeared. It's a long time to bear a grudge. He might not even still be alive."

"Very true. So this attack is more likely to be someone recent, like you said."

"Yeah."

He sat quietly for a minute, digesting this. "This

computer searching that you do, Izzy. Should I be calling you Miss Marple? Or would Lisbeth Salander be more appropriate?"

"Neither. It started as more of a hobby than anything serious."

"Started?"

"In London. I searched for information about men— potential boyfriends—for a couple of friends. I'm hoping to keep doing it as a part-time business."

He gave me a suspicious look. "Does that mean you've been doing your dragon tattoo thing on me?"

"No. But I probably should, just to rule you out of the police investigation." I pressed my lips together to stop the smile that was brewing. "And I can check out the skeletons in your closet."

Craig pulled at the collar of his jacket. "Well, you'll have a hard time of that. There's no room for anything else in my closet because of all the tweed they make me wear."

That made me laugh. "After that I should check out everyone else who might have had reason to hurt Hamish. Will you help me make a list? I can make a start tonight when I get home."

He checked his watch. "Aye, I could. But then we should go and move Eagle, before you head back down the road."

———

PARKING his ancient green Landrover beside my lorry, Craig killed the engine and jumped out. Before I'd even got the passenger door properly open, he was round at my side and reaching for my arm.

"I'm not an invalid, you know." I smiled to let him know I was teasing.

"I know. But it gives me an excuse to hold your hand."

A quick glance at the stable entrance told me that Constable Jobsworth had been replaced by a male policeman, so there was nobody to heap judgement on me or hex me with the evil eye just for being friendly with someone of the opposite gender. I laced my fingers into Craig's, mentally thumbing my nose at PC Adamson.

Craig was still holding my hand a couple of minutes later when we arrived at Eagle's paddock. Back in London, I'd been so independent—and so busy—I think I scared off potential suitors. And even when someone had been interested, like maybe a work colleague, my head ruled my heart and immediately scotched anything unwise or illogical.

So it had been a long time, a *very* long time, since I'd had a man worry about me, or treat me like I was special. It was nice. For a change. Although I wouldn't want to be treated like a feeble female *all* of the time.

Eagle and the girls had settled down and were grazing quietly, but the mares were eating the grass at the other side of the fence from him, almost close enough to touch noses. "Aww, isn't that sweet," I said, taking out my phone to snap a photo that I could show Lady Letham later on.

Craig gave me a cheeky grin. "So that idea of mine to put them in beside each other was a good one, was it?"

"Yeah. Let's just hope they're as friendly when they're all in the same field."

"There's no time like the present," Craig said, unhooking the head collar.

"Can you give me a minute?" I held up a finger, then walked over to the stallion. Taking a deep breath, I planted my feet securely—just in case—and placed a hand on his shoulder.

Nothing.

Maybe I'm not focussed enough. Letting out the breath, I used that to calm my mind, waited a moment, then reached out to Eagle again.

Still nothing.

Maybe the last time had been an aberration. *Or maybe you just imagined it.*

"What's that you're up to?" Craig asked. "Are you after doing some horse whispering or something?"

I thought about trying to obfuscate, but in my experience the truth was often less believable than fiction. "Trying to. But it's not working," I said with a smile.

"The next thing, you'll be joining the Horseman's Guild."

"The Horseman's Guild?" Giving the stallion a pat, I stepped closer to Craig.

"Have you no' heard o' them? They're a group of men up here in the north east who fancy themselves as horse experts. They say they've got some magic word that only members know, and that it will calm any horse."

My eyebrows disappeared somewhere up under my fringe. "Really? I've not heard of them." I gave him a sideways look. "Maybe I should try and join."

Craig made a face. "I'm no' sure they let women in. Misogyny still rules in the old trade guilds, I'm afraid."

"Are *you* a member?"

"No, no. It's not my kind of thing. Anyway, I think you have to be asked to join." He shrugged. "And I don't think my face would fit."

"That might change if you take over as the boss here." I waved an arm in the direction of the stables.

Craig clipped the head collar on Eagle and led him towards the gate to the mares' field. "That's no' going to happen," he said emphatically.

I frowned after him. *Does he mean he's not going to be boss, or not going to join the guild?* I wasn't sure he would be right, on either count.

———

WE LEFT Eagle and the mares 'getting to know each other better' as Craig put it, and walked over to my lorry. When we got there, his face turned serious. "So, Izzy, when will I see you again?"

By this time, I was standing beside him, surrounded by his sandalwood scent and masculine pheromones. My heart began to beat a little faster. "Soon, no doubt. After all, you made sure I'd have to come back in three weeks to collect the mares."

His eyes twinkled. "Aye. There was method in my madness." Placing a finger under my chin, he angled my face up for a kiss.

"Mr MacDonald!" A rasping voice came from nowhere.

Craig let go of me like I was poker-hot, spun on his heel and peered through the hedge behind us. "Mrs Douglas." His face sobered. "Can I just say, I'm right sorry about Hamish. You must be beside yourself."

On the other side of the hedge bordering the parking area stood Hamish's wife, one hand full of roses, the other holding pruning shears. Her eyes were red-rimmed and her face pale, contrasting with the dark green Barbour jacket covering her shoulders. She shook her head sadly. "I am, but I just had to get out and *do* something. The house feels like a mausoleum."

"Have you got any company? Did your daughter come down?" Craig started to walk around the corner towards her garden gate, and I followed.

Mrs Douglas joined us at the other side of the white-painted picket gate. Closer-up, you could see the strain lines on her face, and the dry skin on her nose, probably from being blown incessantly. She certainly looked more like a grieving widow than a calculating murderess. *Maybe it wasn't the wife who dunnit after all.*

"Laura is on her way. Mrs Fisher came over with some soup and scones, sat with me for a while. But then that nice policeman came, so she went back off home." She nodded at the house next door. "After he left, I was so…" She swallowed. "I needed to get outside and keep my hands busy." Distractedly, she waved her secateurs at the garden. "There's always something to do out here." Then her eyes focussed on us again, and she frowned. "Did I see you with Eagle a minute ago?"

Craig's head jerked back at the change of topic. "Aye, we just moved him to a new paddock."

Her forehead creased. "Did the police say it was okay?"

"The police?" Involuntarily, I glanced across at the policeman at the stable yard who seemed more interested in watching the horses cavorting about, and was ignoring us.

"Seeing as the horse is evidence."

My heart plummeted. "It was *Eagle* that kicked Hamish?" I asked, aghast. *Maybe I didn't imagine that vision Eagle showed me, after all.*

Mrs Douglas' lips pursed. "Aye. Couldn't believe it when I found him."

"*You* found him? Oh, that must've been awful for you." It seemed that I'd taken over the questioning.

Mrs Douglas nodded slowly. "I went to the stables after I spoke to you in the pub last night. That's where he was, all…" Her eyes brimmed with tears, and she pulled a damp, lace-edged handkerchief from her pocket. "Sorry," she said, dabbing at her face with the hanky.

"Don't apologise, it's totally understandable." I said. "So he was in Eagle's stable?"

"Yes," she sniffed. "He used to check the horses last thing every night and then walk to the pub for a dram. I'd pick him up there later." She shook her head sadly. "I phoned the doctor straight away I found him, but there was nothing to be done." A tear rolled down her cheek.

"I'm so sorry. I only met him briefly, but he seemed like —" I wracked my brains, trying to think of something nice to say about her late husband. "—a great horseman."

"They were his life. Especially Eagle. That big lump was his favourite." At this, her eyes filled with tears again. "I just don't understand how the boy would have hurt him. Especially if..."

Craig put a hand on her shoulder. "Nor do I, Mrs D. It's no' like Eagle at all."

But I was still frowning at her last words. "Especially if...?" I prompted.

She blotted her eyes with the white cotton. "If he wasn't well," she completed the sentence.

"He wasn't well?" I felt like a parrot, repeating her last words again and again.

"From the bite. The spider bite."

"A spider bite?" This time it was Craig doing the parrot thing. He knitted his brows. "But I dinnae think that spider bites are dangerous."

Lifting a thin shoulder, she sniffed. "It was some fancy foreign one, or so the policeman said. Probably came from the supermarket on some fruit. Paralyses you within fifteen minutes." Her face crumpled, and I put a hand on her arm.

"I'm sure the police will get to the bottom of it soon." I glanced across at Craig. "And we'll do everything we can to help."

She shook her head sadly. "There's nothing to be done. I just have to get over it." A tear rolled down her cheek. "A tragic accident, he called it. There'll be an inquest, of course, but it seems like the police have their answers."

A roar of engine noise drifted on the wind, coming from the estate road. The mechanical sound was rather obvious in this quiet area where the only real noise was the occasional blackbird chittering a warning, or the wind soughing through the pine trees.

Mrs Douglas gave a wan smile. "Maybe that's Laura." She checked her watch. "She's made good time if it is."

Moments later, a sporty blue BMW swung round the corner and growled to a stop outside the cottage. Inside was a forty-ish woman with her black hair swept into a stylish knot at the back of her neck, red lipstick accentuating her lips and dark shades covering her eyes. In her dark suit and white shirt, she looked like I did, just a few months ago—like she'd only moments ago left her desk at some high-powered job in the city.

I stuck my hands in my pockets and gave Craig a quick look from under my lashes.

He took the hint. "Okay now, we'll leave you in peace, Mrs D." He raised a hand in farewell. "Just let me know if you are needing anything. Anything at all. You've got my number."

———

WITH MRS DOUGLAS occupied with welcoming her daughter, Craig walked me back to the truck and carried on where he'd left off with my goodbye kiss. Uninterrupted, this time.

Ten minutes later—or maybe it was fifteen, I kind of lost track—with my toes still tingling and my pulse almost back to normal, I was in the lorry and driving back to Glengowrie.

There was so much to think about, I didn't know where to start. Who'd have thought, when I blithely drove up here yesterday afternoon that I'd have met a dishy royal employee, a hunky policeman... and a grieving widow.

That last thought gave me pause. I thought back to what Mrs D had said about the spider. *Was it really an accident?* I'd heard of foreign spiders coming in on bunches of bananas. If that was the case, then Hamish's death would be bad luck like the police said, not murder like I'd thought.

I tapped a finger on the steering wheel while I thought that scenario through. If the spider bite had made him collapse in Eagle's stable, then the horse may have got a fright and somehow ended up standing on him.

But what about Eagle's vision? I'd got so caught up with Mrs Douglas and then Craig that I'd forgotten about that. Did I *really* get a psychic message from a horse? I knew there were some people in the horse world who called themselves horse whisperers and said that horses 'spoke' to them, but I'd always been sceptical about that, assuming they were charlatans who were really good at reading the owners'—and the horses'—body language. So did I just imagine it?

Of course, if Craig's Horseman's Guild weren't merely grown-up boys playing at secret societies, maybe horse whispering was actually a thing and my imagination hadn't been playing tricks. *But why now?* Why would I suddenly get a message from a horse for the first time at the grand old age of twenty-eight? It didn't seem likely.

I shook my head. *Maybe it was simply a tragic accident after all.*

CHAPTER TEN

I ENDED up going back to Balmoral sooner than I expected.

Two days later, when I'd just about got back into the routine at Glengowrie, I got a phone call from Craig. We'd texted a few times since my visit, so it wasn't entirely unexpected, but the fact that it was a phone call took me a little by surprise. I was also sitting on Leo at the time, so it meant trying to ride one-handed while not dropping the phone in the other. Juggling was never my strong suit.

"Hey Izzy, how's things?"

"Fine thanks. Just schooling Leo at the minute. You okay?"

"Aye, I'm fine thanks. But——" In the pause that followed I could almost hear him running a hand through his hair.

My heart sank. *This doesn't sound like it's going to be good news.*

"It's just——with all the shenanigans going on in the paddock, Allegra has lost a shoe and I'm afraid she's looking a bit sore on that foot."

"Oh. Okay." *Could be worse.* "It's fine to get your farrier out if that's what you were checking. Just get him to bill Lady L."

"Well, you see, that's the problem. He's not back in the

area till next week. Might yours be able to pop up and put it back on?"

Leo stamped a foot impatiently, so I squeezed with my calves to ask him to walk on. "Sorry, I'll need to go. But I'll ask him and let you know soon as."

"Okay. I'll speak with you later."

Just before I clicked the phone off and stuffed it back into my pocket, I thought I heard the sound of him blowing me a kiss. Even if I imagined it, it made me smile for the rest of Leo's training session. *It's the little things.*

Half an hour later, in the gap between riding Leo and working with Merlin, I was frowning, not smiling.

Our farrier, Will Thomson-Bond, who I'd only met once, had unfortunately strained his back and been signed off for a week. The rounded vowels of his West Country accent seemed overly loud on the phone. "But him's okay, my lovely. That Richard Mortimer is doing all my 'orses in the meantime. He'll see you right."

I blinked. Looked like the urban cowboy was going to get his way after all, and get us as a client, albeit temporarily.

"Well, you *did* say you'd give him a try," Trinity reminded me when I came off the phone to Will.

"True." The eager expression on her face gave me an idea. "D'you want to phone him? See how quickly he can fit Allegra in. His card's on the table in the tack room."

She beamed. "Sure thing, boss."

"I thought I told you not to call me…" I tailed off with a sigh as she disappeared into the tack room. There was no point in remonstrating with empty air.

At lunchtime, once I'd finished working the horses, I phoned Craig back. "Our farrier's off sick," I told him. "But that Richard Mortimer is covering for him, and he can fit Allegra in tomorrow at two o'clock."

He exhaled loudly. "Och, would you believe it! That's

about the only time tomorrow that I can't manage. I've a meeting up at the castle at two." There was a pause. "I could ask Stan to hold the mare for you?"

Creepy Stan. *Ugh.* "Let me see if I can organise things here so I can do it myself." At least that would let me check up on the Lone Ranger and see his work in person.

"Well, okay. But only if you let me take you for coffee after."

That put the smile back onto my face, and I went around for the rest of the day doing what Trinity called 'my Cheshire Cat impersonation'.

———

"Just take 'er out here into the laneway an' I'll do 'er there. It'll be less stony for 'er there than in the yard," Richard called over to me as he lugged his heavy equipment from his van in the Balmoral stables car park towards the fields.

Fortunately he couldn't see the surprise on my face. *Didn't expect him to be that thoughtful.* Although, true to form with most farriers I'd ever encountered, he'd been half an hour late for our appointment. So maybe not *that* thoughtful.

A couple of minutes later I had Allegra caught and led her into the path where Richard was waiting. Behind me in the paddock, Daisy and Eagle had their heads down, happily munching on the lush grass, seemingly unbothered that their friend had gone and that the heavy grey clouds overhead were promising rain.

Richard motioned to a piece of orange baler twine looped round one of the fence posts. "Tie 'er to that. She'll be done in no time."

I did as he asked and handed him the lost shoe that Craig had left hanging on the gatepost.

"Lovely jubley." Taking it from me, Richard bent over and

lifted her foot, checking that the shoe still fitted properly. "We'll 'ave this back on in two shakes." Standing up, he patted her shoulder and leaned over his toolbox to pick up his hammer and some nails.

A loud snorting diverted my attention to the paddock, just in time to see Eagle standing up on his hind legs, front legs waving in the air, neck arched and nostrils flaring.

Richard straightened, fist on his hip and a frown creasing his brow. "What's up wiv 'im?"

"I'm not sure. I'll go check." Leaving Allegra tied up, I hurried over to the stallion. Grabbing a head collar from where it was hung on the fence, I opened the gate and approached Eagle, who now had all four feet on the ground but was still staring fixedly at Allegra, every muscle in his body quivering. *Perhaps he's got separation anxiety,* I thought, sending out soothing vibes. *He must really like the mare.*

My calming attitude seemed to help, and it let me quickly clip the head collar onto the stallion who was still tense but less angry looking. Putting a hand on his neck, I channelled placidity, hoping to calm him further.

Instead, I got another vision.

We were still in the stable, with a strange, musky smell filtering through the air, and only faint moonlight to see by. But this time there were *two* shadowy men, arguing angrily. One was smaller—Hamish, I assumed—and the other bigger. In silhouette, the taller man appeared to be wearing a hat with a brim, and it was this man that was causing Eagle's intense feelings of fear and anger.

Almost as quickly as the vision had appeared, it vanished again, leaving me mentally reeling, the hand on the stallion's neck helping to hold me upright as much as calming him.

It took a few seconds for me to get myself together, but fortunately Eagle remained quiet beside me while I gathered my wits. He nuzzled my hand, almost as if he was glad to have shared his memory with me—for I was sure it was real, this time, and not my imagination. There was so much emotion attached, I couldn't have made it up. It affected me right to my core.

Blinking, I looked back across the paddock to check Allegra was okay with Richard, only to spot Craig, who had appeared around the corner of the stable block and was walking towards the farrier, Jet at his heels.

The breath stopped in my throat. *Was it him in the vision?* As usual, Craig had his baseball cap on, brim to the front. And he was certainly taller than Hamish.

Ice trickled down my spine, making me shiver. Could Craig—the lovely man with the mesmerising green eyes— really have killed his boss? And then somehow have hurried away from the stables, met up with me at the pub, and...

My cheeks flushed as I remembered what had happened in the dark outside the guest house. Was that why I couldn't imagine Craig as a murderer? My heart sank. *And was he only being nice to me so he'd have an alibi?*

As I stood motionless beside the stallion, my thoughts in a whirl, Craig spotted me across the paddock and raised a hand in greeting. Keeping my head down, I pretended I hadn't noticed him and busied myself running a hand down the stallion's legs, checking he hadn't strained anything with his antics. It felt churlish, but I just couldn't trust myself to respond to Craig right now, not while I was having these awful suspicions about him.

"Was it him, boy?" I whispered, stroking the stallion's shoulder, my back to the others in the lane. There was still tension in the muscles under his skin, but he was calmer than a few minutes before. "If you tell me, I can let the police know."

Then I almost laughed, as the absurdity of that last statement hit me. *How* would I inform the police? "Officer Night's

Watch, it wasn't an accident, Hamish was killed. And I know who the murderer is, because a horse told me. In a vision." Yeah, that would go down well. Not. They would send unsmiling men with a padded jacket and a little yellow van to collect me, and that would be the last I'd see of daylight for a while. I grimaced. *That won't work, Paterson. You'll need to think of another plan.*

Pursing my lips, I puffed out a breath. So, even if Eagle showed me the murderer, I couldn't tell the police, or they'd think I was nuts. I clenched my fists. *I'll just have to find other evidence then.* Decision made, I nodded imperceptibly, then slipped the stallion's head collar off and gave him a pat. "I'll need to set Gremlin on him," I muttered conspiratorially.

"What's that you're saying about gremlins?" Craig appeared at Eagle's other shoulder, and I nearly jumped out of my skin.

"Oh! You gave me a fright," I said, dropping the head collar in my fluster. Picking it up gave me an excuse to delay replying, and time to think of a decent answer. "I was just saying it must have been gremlins that set him off. Eagle, I mean," I added, patting his shoulder again. "He took a right funny turn when he discovered Allegra was missing."

"So Richard said." Swiping the cap off his head, Craig rubbed his forehead with the back of his hand, squinting in the sunlight. "My meeting at the castle finished early." He jerked his head northwards. "Would you want to go for a coffee? Then I can tell you all about it?"

I checked my watch, using it as another excuse to delay replying. What could I say? From being excited about seeing Craig again, I was now feeling mistrustful and suspicious. Should I make my excuses and head back to Glengowrie, or should I meet up with him and pump him for information?

"I can only spare a little while," I said, deciding that I could do some investigating in person now, and use Gremlin later. "The farrier was late, so it's set me back." I motioned with my chin at the farrier and Allegra. "I'll need to square up with him and put the mare back in the field first."

"Of course, of course. Shall we go to the café again?"

"Okay," I said. Surely I'd be safe enough in a public place, even if he *was* the killer?

He dangled his keys. "Would you want a lift?"

I shook my head. "I'll follow you in my car once Allegra's done. That way I can make a quick getaway after." *And that way I can avoid being in a confined space with a possible murderer.* There was no harm in being careful, was there?

———

CRAIG PUT his elbows on the table and looked at me over the top of his coffee cup. "So I couldn't tell you on the phone, but the estate manager called me up to the castle for a meeting, and, would you believe it, he said that, subject to the Queen's approval, they're going to make me Stud Manager to replace Hamish!" His smile slowly grew, reaching from one ear to the other and lighting up his whole face.

"That's great!" I said, finding his enthusiasm rather infectious, even though his news gave him prime reason to murder his ex-boss. "But you thought that might happen?"

"Well, aye, since I was Hamish's second-in-command. But they could always have advertised the job outside. I mean, I've only been here a couple of years, so they mightn't have thought I had enough experience."

"True. Well, congratulations, then," I said, raising my coffee cup and clinking it against his. I had no real appetite to drink it, though. All this suspicion was wreaking havoc with my insides, and I was finding it hard to behave normally around Craig. Acting had never been my strong point. "Is the Queen's approval just a formality? Like parliament? Surely she delegates stuff like this. Otherwise she'd be doing nothing but paperwork."

"Aye, but she's more involved with the stud, since horses play such a big part in her life. She used to meet with Hamish once or twice a year, to go over the breeding plans. So I'm no' sure if it's a formality or not." An anxious look flitted across his face.

"Have you met her before?"

He nodded. "When she's been up in the summer, aye, once or twice. I've saddled her horse ready for her to ride, held it while she got on." He could see the next question in my face. "She was okay wi' me, I suppose. Even cracked a wee joke, one time."

"That's good then. But surely the new job means your duties will change?" I asked, trying to keep him talking.

"Aye." He set his cup down and stared at his drink for a moment before meeting my eyes again. "I'll have more to do wi' the stud, and less time up the hill." His mouth set in a line.

"Will you miss it?"

"I suppose I will, yes. I like being up there wi' the garrons. Even when the weather's bad it's still spectacular up there."

"I can imagine."

Craig caught my hand across the table. "You should come up wi' me sometime. Join in one of the shoots."

With a shudder, I shook my head and snatched my hand away. "I couldn't do that. I'm okay knowing in theory that it happens, I know that deer numbers need controlling. But I wouldn't want to see it in person."

Looking a little crestfallen, Craig nodded slowly. "Okay, that's fair enough. Some of the guns can be a bit boorish. Or boring. So at least you're saved from that." His face brightened. "We could just go for a hill walk together on a day off. Conachcraig has some lovely views over Lochnagar.

Or Craigendarroch is an easy walk through an old oak wood."

I nodded noncommittally. "I love those Scottish names. They just trip so easily off your tongue. Are they Gaelic?"

"Yes, probably. My mother has the Gaelic, but I'm afraid I don't speak it."

"The Gaelic," I repeated, mimicking his lilt. "So quaint!"

"You'll be taken for a Sassenach if you carry on like that," he teased.

I snorted, then remembered that I was supposed to be interrogating him about the murder. "So does the new job mean you'll be moving into Hamish's cottage at the stables?"

"Och, no, I wouldnae do that to Mrs Douglas. She loves thon garden. No, I'll stay where I am, it's no' far from the stables and big enough for me and Jet." He dropped his hand under the table to scratch the top of the Labrador's head. "If I ever needed somewhere larger," he gave me a significant look as he said this, "I could ask the estate manager to move me. But I'm fine for now."

Hmmm. It seemed that wanting a better house wasn't his reason for murder. Then something snagged at my brain. "You live near the stables? But..." I visualised the route from the B&B, through the main gate and on to the stables, "it must've taken you ages to walk home the other night after the pub?"

"No' really." He leaned forward conspiratorially. "Only the locals know this, but, not far from the pub, there's a set of stepping stones across the river. It's a back way into the estate, and it's a short-cut home for me."

"That's handy." My mind whirred. What other motives might he have? "The new job must mean you'll get paid more? Especially if they're not giving you a better house."

Pulling the baseball cap off his head, Craig set it on the table and mussed his curls with his right hand. "Aye, I suppose I might. I never thought to ask. Maybe I should find myself an expensive hobby." I got another sideways look at this point. "Right now, most of my salary goes to savings, what with accommodation being provided by the estate. All I've got left to pay for is diesel for the landy, food, and clothes. And my sister gets me a discount on those at the department store where she works."

"Your sister?"

"Aye, she's a personal shopper over in Glasgow."

Personal shopper. That would explain his good taste in clothes. But if it wasn't for more money or a bigger house, why on earth would Craig have murdered Hamish?

Prestige maybe? "I suppose it'll be similar for me, in my new job, although I have to buy feed for my own horses and pay vet bills and show entries as well. I've not been here long enough to get a real handle on my budget. Down in London everything was so expensive. And I had Leo on full livery, which cost a fortune."

"Maybes I should get a horse." Craig's face took on a far-away look.

I chuckled. "That would certainly count as an expensive hobby." Tilting my head to the side, I asked, "What kind of horse would you get?"

"Och, one for hacking I suppose. I like getting out and about for a ramble in the countryside. Maybe a bit of jumping, if I had time."

"D'you not get to ride the horses here, though? The garrons?"

His finger traced the outline of one of the squares on the tartan tablecloth. "Aye, you're right. We have to keep them trained and exercised for the royals and their friends, when they visit. If I think about it like that, I dinnae really need a horse."

"With your new job you'll have more to do with the stud

horses like Eagle, won't you?" I watched his face for any flicker of guilt.

"True." He remained distracted, but there was no trace of bad conscience.

"Will you get to represent the stud in public? Shows maybe? Or trade fairs?" Perhaps prestige was a motive.

Craig's hand stilled and his eyes widened. "The Highland!" He almost looked shocked. "You've just reminded me. Hamish always enters..." he corrected himself, "entered the ponies for the Royal Highland Show in Edinburgh in June."

"That's good. Isn't it?" I added, noticing that his face had paled, making his freckles more obvious.

"Aye. No. Maybe. Y'see, it'll fall to me to do the showing now." He grimaced. "I could be doing wi'out it."

I took a long pull from my coffee to give me breathing space to think, surveying Craig from under my eyelashes.

None of my ideas for motive were panning out here. So either Craig was innocent and I'd interpreted Eagle's vision wrongly, or he was guilty but I just hadn't worked out the reason why. I was starting to lean towards the former, but I was worried it was my heart, not my head, that was leading the way.

What is it they always say in crime shows? Innocent until proven guilty? So perhaps I should treat him as innocent for now. I sat back in my chair. "I can help you. Groom for you or whatever. I think Lady L has entered some of her horses, and she was talking about me getting a late entry for Leo. So we'll be there anyway."

Relief washed over Craig's features. "That would be magic! I'll be fine with just a little more experience. It's the thought of exhibiting on behalf of the Queen that worries me. I wouldnae want to let her down."

Definitely not prestige as a motive then. "We can have some practice beforehand. At home. Or you can take some of our horses to a smaller show where it's not so high-powered and you're not representing the Queen."

He smiled his big smile again and held out a hand. "That's a deal!"

––––––––

DRIVING BACK TO GLENGOWRIE, the grey landscape flashing by my windows reflected my mood. Outside, the clouds had got heavier and the air darker, almost buzzing with anger, so much so that it felt like the gloom of a winter evening, even though it was only late afternoon in May.

But the long drive gave me time to mull over the mystery of Hamish's death some more. On the way from the café to the car I'd finally remembered to get Craig to give me a list of suspects from the estate. Unfortunately, his input didn't add much to the list I'd already concocted on my own.

I didn't tell him, but Craig was still my number one suspect, lack of motive notwithstanding. Mrs D had to be a suspect too, although if she did it, she should get an Oscar for her acting abilities. Stan was on the list, since he would have had opportunity, but I hadn't yet found a motive. Craig suggested adding the child catcher gamekeeper, who similarly had opportunity but no obvious motive. In fact, anyone on the estate could have had opportunity, in theory. So maybe I needed to hunt harder for motive.

Was there more to find out about Hamish, which might provide clues to a reason he'd been killed? Perhaps I could've questioned his wife, pumped her for information. But it would have been rather insensitive at this time. If only Hamish had a biography or something...

In a flash of inspiration, I remembered my great-uncle's cremation some years ago, and all the things I'd discovered about him during the eulogy: that he'd been crew on one of the ships at Dunkirk during the war, and later had been Harbour Master at Newcastle before retiring to tend his large vegetable garden.

I need to attend Hamish's funeral. And check out the newspaper for an obituary—as a military man and senior employee of the Queen, he would likely be commemorated in print.

But... At the funeral and in an obituary, people would only say positive things about the man, no matter how unpopular he was.

What I *really* needed was to find someone at Balmoral who was more of a gossip, so I'd find out who might have a grudge against Hamish. Maybe I shouldn't have been so keen to avoid Mrs Beaton at the B&B. No doubt she'd have lots of stories, if I could just stop her from picking on me and Craig. But it was hard for me to spend long with an intense person like her, being more of an introvert.

Perhaps I could get Trinity involved? She was so good with people. *Could she be like Watson to my Sherlock? My side-kick who would interview suspects while I checked out their alibis on the computer?*

With a sudden metallic drumming that almost made me jump out of my skin, the heavens opened like a sluice, and rain poured down from the heavy sky, hammering against the windscreen of my car so hard that the window wipers could hardly keep up. Slowing to a crawl, I had to divert all my attention to peering through the curtain of rain bouncing off the road ahead.

Hamish's murderer would have to wait.

CHAPTER ELEVEN

By the time I reached the southern edge of Glengowrie, it was still raining—hard—and I'd had to concentrate so hard on the driving that a headache was brewing. But when I turned the last corner to approach the main street of the little town, I was met by flashing blue lights and men in fluorescent yellow jackets who were diverting the traffic.

"Canny get into the centre, Miss," said a policeman when I rolled my window down. "The river's burst its banks and there's a foot of water on the road. Ye'll need tae go round the long way." He pointed an arm up the road round the back of the town.

My throat constricted. "Do you know if Kirk Wynd is affected? We live there."

Bushy grey eyebrows drew together. "Give me a minute to check." Pulling open the collar of his high-vis jacket, he spoke into his radio, which replied with a buzz of static and unintelligible sentences. Then he turned back to me. "Not quite yet, but the water's rising quickly so it won't be long before it's evacuated. If you want to get your stuff out, you'd better be quick. You'll get in from Riverside Way on the west side. And you'll need somewhere to go afterwards."

I grimaced. I had an idea about that, but it wouldn't be ideal. "D'you think I've time to collect my flatmate first? She's at Glengowrie House."

He glanced up at the sky, then checked his watch. "I reckon twenty minutes, half-hour max before they close off Kirk Street. So you'd better be quick."

———

WITH A SCREECH of tyres and a spray of gravel, I arrived back at Glengowrie House some minutes later, parked my car, and scooted into the stable yard, holding a jacket over my head.

I almost bumped into Trinity, who was ushering a rather bedraggled Dancer into his stable. Dancer was the young skewbald Warmblood gelding I'd bought with my final bonus from Bleubank, and I thought he had the talent to become a great dressage horse. All the other stables appeared to be full, and a couple of long noses poked over half-doors to check on the new arrival.

"We need to get away to the flat, Trin." I said, clutching the stable door. "There's flooding in the town, apparently the river's burst its banks and Kirk Street will be closed any minute." I started shrugging my arms into the sleeves of my jacket. "Let's go, so we can get some of our things."

Trinity's face turned white. "The river?" She fumbled the head collar off Dancer's head with fingers that appeared to have turned to ice. "But..."

Her legs started to buckle, so I grabbed a bucket and opened the door just in time to turn the bucket upside down and give her something to sit on. "What's wrong?" I asked. In the months I'd known her, I'd never seen Trinity looking anything but competent and together.

Crouched on the feed bucket, she had her head in her hands and her elbows on her knees. She shook her head then looked at me with sudden hope in her expression. "Maybe it's not that bad?"

I grimaced. "The policeman said a foot of water."

Her face crumpled again. "Oh my," she wailed, scrunching her eyes closed.

"I don't mean to be insensitive," I said, checking my watch, "but if we don't leave now, we won't be able to get anything, and we'll be stranded here in what we're wearing." I waved a hand at my damp jeans, soggy jacket and muddy boots.

"Sorry," she said. "It's just... I can't swim. I'm terrified of water. This is like all my worst nightmares come true."

Scrunching my nose, I puffed out a breath. "You'll be all right. I can swim, and I got lifesaving badges at school. We'll be fine."

Brown eyes gazed up at me. "You sure?"

"Sure I'm sure." I released the latch on the stable door, hoping she'd take the hint.

With a burst of energy, she stood, and almost knocked me over in her rush to get out. "Okay, let's go."

Grabbing the bucket and giving Dancer an apologetic look, I hurried after her. "Wait!" I shouted. "We'll go in my car. It'll be better than yours in this weather."

Almost at her car, Trinity stopped, with the Mini Cooper key fob in her outstretched hand. She looked from her low-slung green coupe to my four-wheel-drive with its good ground clearance and meaty tyres, like someone assessing livestock at an auction. "Okay," she said, spinning on her heel and hurrying to the passenger side of my Volkswagen—another purchase from my Bleubank bonus.

Rain spattered on my head and drips from the end of my pony tail were making their icy way down the back of my neck like wraiths at Halloween. I beeped my car open and rummaged in the back for a baseball cap, before jumping into the driver's seat and racing off like the hounds of hell were after us.

————

WE'D ONLY TRAVELLED about a quarter of a mile when a glimpse of something white by the side of the road had me diving for the brake pedal. Like a learner driver practicing emergency braking, I screeched the car to a stop, my heart suddenly in my mouth.

"What is it?" Trinity asked, scanning the road ahead. There were no old ladies waiting to cross, or fallen branches blocking the carriageway.

I didn't take the time to answer. Instead, I flicked the hazard lights on, scrambled to undo my seatbelt, then cautiously opened the door and stepped out into the downpour, arm outstretched.

The white and brown terrier that I'd seen on the railway path the other day sat hunched and miserable at the side of the road, sheltering under some overhanging trees.

It took some patience—and me getting soaked to the skin —but a few minutes later I finally had the dog in my arms and was back in the car, emanating triumph. "Can you take him?" I asked Trinity as a car overtook us, headlamps glaring through the rain.

I handed the bedraggled beast to her, then started the engine. But a glance in the rearview mirror showed an empty road behind, so I took a moment to give the dog's head a quick rub. Big brown eyes turned to look up to me, then a pink tongue popped out and gave me a lick on the hand.

"Aww, he's saying thanks for getting him out of the rain." Trinity's eyebrows scrunched together. "Or is it a she?" She took a quick look. "Girl."

Got that wrong.

Using her fingers to press carefully all over the dog's body, Trinity checked for cuts or breaks. "Seems to be okay, just a bit thin. And wet." She looked across at me and frowned. "Maybe she's just lost. Although..." she almost muttered to herself, "she's not got a collar on."

"I saw her a few days ago when I was riding, but I couldn't catch her. It was the same day that farrier, Richard, arrived at the yard to see us, so I forgot to tell you. Which means she's been missing for a while now. We should take her to the vet's surgery, check if anyone's reported a dog missing."

Glancing at the digital clock on the dashboard of the car, Trinity shook her head. "They'll be shut by the time we finish at the flat. It's after five."

"Okay." I put the car into gear. "Let's take her with us for now, and we can check with the vet in the morning." I ruffled the dog's ears before switching off the hazard lights and pulling away. "Whoever owns such a little sweetie should be tearing their hair out worrying where she's got to."

———

IT WAS ONLY a short distance from there to the town, and soon we were approaching Riverside Way. My heart sank at the sight that greeted us. *Maybe I shouldn't have stopped for the dog.* But one glance at her cute little face dispelled that thought.

To the right of the road, and dangerously close to the kerb, muddy brown water swirled past and on towards the grey stone buildings of the town, litter and tree branches sailing along like ships at a regatta. Listing at a drunken angle, a litter bin bobbed slowly in from the right, then picked up speed as it joined the main confluence. In the passenger seat, Trinity whimpered, and drew her knees up towards her chest.

There was no river any more, no banks or roads. Just a field of water with a hump-backed bridge poking forlornly above the tumult, white-capped standing waves rolling against its upstream pillars. With every flick of the windscreen wipers the water level seemed to rise a centimetre.

A different policeman barred the way at this end of town, his yellow jacked flaring in the headlights.

I glanced across at Trinity. Her eyes were bright with tears. Puffing out a heavy breath, I drew the car alongside the policeman and buzzed down the window. "Evening, officer. We," I inclined my head towards Trinity, "live on Kirk Wynd. The policeman at the other side of town said we should be able to get in to pick up some stuff if we were quick? My car is four-wheel-drive."

The black-bearded policeman pressed his lips together, causing his moustache to bristle like a living thing. He glanced over his shoulder, then back at us. "Ye'll need tae be quick, lassie. We've evacuated all the houses within two streets of the river and those roads are closed. Kirk Street will be next." He tapped a finger on the radio handset attached at collarbone height to his yellow jacket. "What's your names and address so I can radio it to the guys in the centre."

Trinity leaned across and gave him our details.

Her tear-streaked face earned a sympathetic look from the copper. "Okay. Check in wi' me on your way out so we know you're safe." He glanced at me. "Have ye somewhere ye can stay tonight? There's some emergency beds at the school gym if ye need it."

"I think so," I answered. I hadn't had time to fill Trinity in on my idea. "We work for Lady Letham, and there's accommodation almost ready above the stables. We'll camp there. Will someone let us know when we can get into the flat again?"

"We can rightly. So where's that you'll be staying?" He pulled a grubby notebook out of his pocket.

"Glengowrie Stables Cottage," I told him.

"Oh, aye." He scribbled it down, then gave us a nod. Fat drops of water splashed to the ground from the peak of his cap. "Off ye get now, ladies. 'Tis not the weather to be driving around. Ten minutes max, then I want ye out of there."

CHAPTER TWELVE

IT FELT like we were aid workers at some natural disaster when we arrived at our flat, settled the dog onto the back seat of the car, then rushed up the stairs, two steps at a time. "I'll get my stuff from the bathroom while you get your things from the bedroom, then we can swap," I suggested, propping the front door open with a heavy boot and grabbing a plastic bag from a hook in the hallway as I passed.

Trinity nodded and whirled off.

With more expediency than science, I swept things off the bathroom shelf, grabbed my shampoo from the shower, then stuffed my sponge bag and a couple of clean towels on top, before heading for the bedroom. "That's the bathroom free," I shouted as I passed through the hall.

Minutes later, I had a bulging suitcase sitting in the hallway and ran to the desk in the lounge to retrieve my computer kit, which fitted into a padded backpack. Then I joined Trinity in the kitchen where she was packing cans and jars into a hessian shopping bag. Stopping for a moment, I chewed my lip. "D'you think we could take the microwave and kettle? Then we'd have something to cook on. Oh, and mugs and plates?"

"And cutlery. And the telly." suggested Trinity. "But maybe we should get the other stuff to the car first before we do that. We can always get take-out if there's not time."

"Okay." I hurried off to the hall, grabbing the first load of bags as I went. When I got to the vehicle, a line of yellow jackets was advancing up Kirk Street. I reckoned I had time for one more trip.

I passed Trinity on the way up the stairs. "One more load," I said, my breathing ragged, "then I think they'll be chasing us out."

"Right," she grunted.

Minutes later, with the microwave, TV and kettle on the back seat alongside the dog, I performed a rather messy u-turn and splashed through the large puddle that had encroached onto Kirk Wind. "We made it," I said, stating the obvious.

"Yeah." Trinity breathed a sigh of relief. "An' you didn't have to life-save me."

I chuckled, then raised a hand at the gaggle of police, who were busy cordoning off Kirk Street. "I guess we'd better phone Lady L and tell her we're moving in. Early."

———

AFTER A DIVERSION to the small supermarket on the northern side of town to pick up some dog food and supplies to cook dinner, and a garage to buy a bag of logs for the fire, we made it back to Glengowrie Stables Cottage.

We dropped the shopping bags on the kitchen floor, then used an old towel to dry the dog before offering her a little food on a saucer. "Don't want to give her too much in case she's not eaten for a while. It might make her sick."

Trinity nodded. "Good point. Shall I put the pizza in the oven?"

"That's an idea. It can cook while we pick up those electric fires from Lady L. Then we shouldn't have to go out again." I looked back down at the dog. The food had disappeared. "I think she liked that." Opening her mouth, the terrier sat down and gave a huge yawn, pink tongue lolling from the side of her mouth. We both laughed. "Someone needs her bed!" I said, leading the way into the lounge area.

I pointed the dog at a cushion on the couch. She jumped up, circled three times, then plopped down with a happy sigh and promptly closed her eyes.

Quickly, I laid the fire, reminded of weekends in my youth when it'd been my job to set the fire in the family lounge. A useful skill, as it turned out, since London was a 'smokeless zone' and Trinity hadn't been in the girl guides, so was clueless when it came to non-electric fires.

Soon the kindling had burned, and flames were licking at the larger pieces of wood. "Won't be long till the room warms up," I said, as my flatmate appeared from the kitchen area. "Shall we go and get that stuff from the big house before it gets too late?"

A few minutes later, I parked the car at the kitchen door of Glengowrie House. In comparison to the grand columns and carved stone at the front, the back was made from plain red sandstone blocks and white-painted sash windows. Presumably this had been the servants' quarters in the old days, and they didn't warrant fancy architecture.

Ursula Harkin, Lady Letham's cook and housekeeper, opened the door to us, accompanied by a waft of warm air and the smell of baking. A small, dumpy woman with curled grey hair, she wore a grey woollen skirt and white blouse under a black apron that was streaked with flour. "Come in, lassies, come in. Get yourselves out of that horrid rain." She ushered us into the large, flagstone floored room.

Two electric fires and an oil-fired radiator were grouped near the door. "Jimmy looked these out for you." Ursula put her hands on her ample hips. "I told herself she should have got the plumber back in this week to connect up the heating so you could move in. But she didn't want to bother him. His mother took a turn and had a spell in the hospital." She raised her hands. "But work still has to be done, doesn't it?" She ploughed on, not waiting for an answer. "Is that all you're needing? Just the heating?"

"And the shower isn't connected up," I said. "But we've got water to the basin and the bath." I moved to the side and picked up the two fires. Trinity hefted the radiator and headed for the car.

Ursula shook her head. "I'll be having a word with the plumber for you. Canny be having you young ladies shivering over there in that draughty house."

"We'll be fine with these," I nodded at the fires, "And the log fire. At least we'll be dry, which is more than we'd have been down in the town."

"Oh, I know, it's terrible, it is. All those houses. All that water. All those poor people."

That reminded me of something. I turned back from the door. "Oh, by the way, we found a stray dog down the town. We've taken her home with us for now and we'll speak to the vet in the morning, but if you hear of anyone who's lost a wee Jack Russell Terrier, will you let us know?"

"Of course I will." Ursula disappeared for a few moments, then ducked out of the kitchen and thrust a tin at me while I was loading the fires into the car. "Here. A cake for you and Miss Trinity. You lassies are far too thin." She patted my arm. "You need some meat on your bones." Without waiting for a reply, she scurried back in out of the rain.

"Thanks," I called after her, but the door was already closed. "Pizza and cake for dinner," I said, handing the tin to Trinity as I clambered into the driver's seat.

"Yum," she said, licking her lips. "That'll be most of the main food groups covered, then, won't it?"

I snorted. "Yeah. Carbohydrate and more carbohydrate."

She lifted a corner of the cake tin lid and peered inside. "There's some strawberry jam in the sponge. So that's us got fruit covered. And tomato and cheese on the pizza, so there's veg and protein." With a wink, she added, "Almost a balanced meal!"

I raised my eyes heavenwards. "At least we're not eating watermelon. Or watercress. Or water chestnut. Or—"

Trinity slapped my arm. "Will you stop with the flooding jokes? You know I'm scared of drowning. Come on, let's get back before the pizza burns. Or before the dog eats it!"

———

NOT ONLY WAS the new flat missing a working shower, it also didn't have a television aerial. Or internet. And we didn't have any DVDs. This would have made for a quiet evening, except that I decided to use Trinity as my 'Watson' and bounce ideas off her about Hamish's murder. Or murder*er*, to be more precise.

"Craig sounds lovely," she said when I told her that Eagle had seemed upset when he appeared. I still hadn't had the courage to tell her about the visions. "I can't imagine it'd be him. Why would he *do* something like that?"

"That's just it. He's the one with the most to gain, so in theory he has the biggest motive. Although, when I questioned him, he didn't seem bothered about getting Hamish's job."

"Well, who else could it be?"

I grimaced. "On the TV it's always the person you'd least suspect. But if you read the newspapers, it's usually a family member. Except his wife is a wee sweetie and doesn't look like she'd hurt a fly. And his daughter wasn't even here—she just arrived, from Glasgow or somewhere."

"What about other people he worked with?"

"Well, there's Slytherin Stan and the Child Catcher."

Her eyebrows disappeared somewhere up under her hairline. "Don't tell me they're making a Disney movie up at the estate?"

I chuckled. "No, just my names for them. Stan is a groom, and the gamekeeper—the one who looks like the Child Catcher from Chitty Chitty Bang Bang—"

"I never saw that one," interrupted Trinity.

"Not even at Christmas time?" My nose wrinkled in surprise.

She shrugged. "We was more into game shows and soaps in our house. Dad never had the patience to sit through a whole film."

"Well, the gamekeeper looks like a beanpole wearing tweed, with a nose that would make Caesar proud. But he only popped in to the yard briefly, and there didn't seem to be any animosity between him and Hamish."

Brow puckering, Trinity took a sip of her tea. "And weren't there anybody else at the stables?"

"Not that I saw." I cradled my coffee mug while I thought back. "There were three guys at the B&B who were part of the next day's shooting party I think. But they weren't on the estate on the Monday as far as I'm aware."

"What else do you know about Hamish, then? Were he involved in anything else that could give him enemies?"

"It's funny you should ask that. I did some research on him and discovered that he saved the Queen's life back in 1984 when he was in the Household Cavalry. Some guy shot at her during the Trooping the Colour, and Hamish and a policeman overpowered him. But the guy would be in his fifties now, so I can't see why he would wait till now to take his revenge."

"Yeah, that would be really weird. Anything else?"

I thought back to Hamish's office at the stud. "He was very tidy. And maybe a councillor or something—there was a photo of him wearing a chain and carrying a staff. I must look that one up."

Trinity's face took on a sly look. "Or you could phone Craig and ask him."

Beside me on the couch, the dog raised her head, opened her mouth in a yawn that showed every one of her little white teeth, got up and turned round three times, then settled herself back down to sleep again. I scratched the back of her neck. "I suppose I could."

My housemate gathered the plates and cups from the low table in front of us and motioned towards the kitchen area. "I'll get on with the washing up while you phone him."

Tactful. But would Craig think I was chasing him if I phoned so soon after seeing him this afternoon? I sighed. I wasn't very good at these dating games. If that's even what it was between us. We'd only shared a couple of meals and a couple of kisses. Did that make him my boyfriend? *Probably not.*

"'Ave you phoned him yet?" questioned a voice from the kitchen.

I rolled my eyes, but pulled my phone out of my pocket. There may not be internet connection here, but at least there was phone signal. And then I gasped. The device showed one bar of wi-fi, labelled 'Lethamor'. We must be picking up the internet from the big house! *Just.*

Instead of phoning Craig and jeopardising... whatever we had, I phoned Mrs H and got the wi-fi password. Using my laptop to investigate was much more in my comfort zone, and I could always phone Craig tomorrow if I needed any further info, couldn't I?

———

After about an hour's internet sleuthing, I'd uncovered further surprising information about Hamish, and an explanation for the strange photo I'd seen in his office.

It turned out that Hamish was Grand Master of a secret society—the one Craig had mentioned—called The Horseman's Guild. Operating mainly in the north-east of Scotland, and reminiscent of the freemasons, the membership consisted of men—it looked to be *only* men—who worked with horses.

The most secret part of their secret society was 'the horseman's word'—a special word that was supposed to calm and tame *any* horse, if only you knew it.

Hmmm. I had my doubts about that. But it explained the photo of Hamish with the tartan and the staff.

It didn't help any with explaining how or why he had died, though. *But maybe some of his colleagues from the guild would know more. Or might hold a grudge.* I stared out the window a moment, eyes fixed on the elegant branches of the oak tree outside, but not really seeing them. *Time for the heavy guns.*

Flexing my fingers, I fired up Gremlin, the app I'd written specifically for burrowing into the deep web, and set it to hunting for more information about the Horseman's Guild membership.

CHAPTER THIRTEEN

I T SEEMED like no time later that I was once more navigating the country roads back to Balmoral. But this time it was a distinctly more sombre affair, as we were on our way to Hamish's funeral.

Lady Letham was in the front seat of my Volkswagen, handbag clutched in her lap with the disabled car pass that Mrs Harkin had remembered at the last minute sticking out of the top. Trinity sat in the back, along with the dog.

We'd had no luck finding out who the animal belonged to, so had taken to calling her Jorja, after one of the characters in CSI, our favourite TV show. She was a sweet and well-mannered thing and seemed quite happy to potter around with us while we worked with the horses.

Strictly speaking, Trinity didn't need to be there, since she'd never met Hamish. But she wanted to come along so she could meet Craig. And I was glad to have her with me. I hoped that, with her superior people-management skills, she could winkle out some gossip about the man.

Lady L was uncharacteristically quiet, staring pensively out of the passenger window at the scenery. I was about to ask if she was okay, when she dabbed a handkerchief at her eyes, then turned to me. "It will be very lovely to see Beverly again, even if the circumstances are not the most conducive to reunions."

"Beverly?" I asked.

"Mrs Douglas. Hamish's dear wife."

"You know her?"

"From the Angus Flower Show. On many occasions, I've presented the prizes, and she regularly wins the cup for the best flower arrangement. She's also a leading light in the Women's Institute. Quite the exceptional lady."

I filed that information away. "Did you know Hamish as well?"

"Somewhat. He is—was," she corrected herself, "not the most... gregarious of men. But a dab hand with the horses."

"I believe he used to be in the Household Cavalry?"

"Yes, I recall hearing something to that effect. And he got a medal from the Falklands War."

"Really? When was that again?"

"Sometime in the eighties? If I recollect correctly, Thatcher was the prime minister."

From the back of the car, Trinity's voice piped up. "Google says 1982."

Scrunching my brows, I caught Trinity's eye in the rear-view mirror. Could there be a murder motive there?

Seeming to understand my look, her shoulders raised. "Bit early?" she mouthed.

She had a point. Like the Marcus Sarjeant incident, surely a war that long ago would have nothing to do with a murder in 2018. I sighed inwardly. *Back to the drawing board.* Or, more accurately, back to the computer investigations.

Gremlin's most recent discoveries had been some details about the horseman's guild committee, including the fact that Oliver Seaforth, the vet, was deputy grand master. I'd also seen documentation that explained how, as Grand Master, Hamish could expect to serve a five-year term, that he had the deciding vote on any resolutions, and executive authority on any spending decisions.

Would that be reason enough for another member to kill him? *Perhaps.* Ghoulish as it might seem, I was hopeful that we might find out more at the funeral.

My musings were interrupted by my employer. "Ladies, I should tell you, in the event that Libby attends poor Hamish's funeral—"

"Will the Queen be there?" Trinity interrupted. "Really?"

"I cannot be sure," Lady Letham continued, "but she occasionally attends funerals of dear friends and esteemed staff. If she *is* there, are you aware of protocol when meeting the Queen?"

I shook my head. "I've never met her. What about you, Trinity?"

"Me either. Waved at her from a street corner in London once with my school when I were a kid. But that's it."

Lady Letham tapped her forefingers together. "Well, the first thing you should know is: never speak to the Queen unless she speaks to you first." As she spoke, her back straightened, as if she was remembering her days as a lady-in-waiting. "And if she does, *do* give her a quick curtsey before you speak. Finally, if need be, you address her as 'Your Majesty' the first time, and then 'ma'am' after that."

"Got it!" said Trinity.

"Thanks," I said. "But I doubt mere plebs like us will get to speak to her."

Little did I know how wrong I would be...

———

THE BIGGEST SURPRISE about Hamish's funeral—apart from the size of the crowd, which was huge considering how grumpy the man was—was that the Queen did, indeed, attend.

As I squeezed my car into the disabled car parking space outside Crathie Church, a spotless burgundy limousine swept past, and drew to a halt near the back of the church.

We all watched in surprise as the chauffeur hurried to open the door, and out stepped Queen Elizabeth, hat and handbag first. Slightly stooped, she wore a monochrome coat and dress, with matching black shoes and gloves.

"Libby!" breathed Lady Letham, bright eyes following the monarch's entourage. "She hasn't aged a day."

Waiting at a side door was the church minister, who greeted the Queen and led her into the church. She was accompanied by another smartly dressed lady, and followed by a couple of men in dark suits, muttering into their shirt sleeves as their eyes darted everywhere.

Once we'd lifted our jaws from where they'd dropped on the ground, we made our way to the front of the church and found Craig hanging around near the porch. The wooden structure looked like it was made out of gingerbread and belonged in a Hansel and Gretel fairytale rather than a Scottish church.

Craig's face lit up when he spotted me. "I saved us some seats," he said, then dipped his head at my boss. "Lady Letham, it's good to see you. Are you keeping well?"

"Why yes, dear boy, thanks for asking."

Obviously they knew each other. I gave Craig a sideways look. I'd need to interrogate him later.

"An' I'm Trinity." My flatmate came forward with her hand outstretched and a wide smile on her face.

"Sorry, I was about to introduce you." My cheeks turned pink. Would Craig be quite so friendly if he knew that I'd had

Gremlin investigating him last night? He'd come out of it with a clear copybook—minimal internet presence and no obvious skeletons in his closet. But it made me feel bad, to be investigating people I was friends with.

Craig clasped Trinity's hand. "It's grand to meet you." He leaned in conspiratorially and arched his eyebrows. "You'll need to be telling me all of herself's secrets."

Trinity pulled a finger and thumb along her mouth. "Me lips are sealed, sorry mate. Girl code."

He lifted a shoulder and made a wry face in my direction. "It was worth a try."

The church was filling up, so Craig led us inside and down to a pew on the right-hand side, Lady Letham's walking stick tapping like a metronome on the red tiled floor.

My eyes were drawn to the impressive arched ceiling, made from a warm-coloured wood, possibly the local Scots pine. With walls made of light grey granite and several large stained-glass windows on either side, the space was bright and warm, even on such a sombre occasion.

The queen and her entourage were seated out of sight in a side aisle at the front of the church. From our vantage point in the middle of the nave, we were surrounded by a sea of black suits and dark coats, a groundswell of muted conversations and the faint smell of mothballs.

Craig leaned in and whispered, "How've you been? All settled in to the new flat?"

"Almost, thanks. We've got a TV aerial now. And the internet got connected up yesterday. But nobody's come forward about the dog yet."

His brow crinkled. "That's a shame. Might you get to keep the beastie?"

"Maybe. Well, yes, I suppose so, if we don't find the owner."

"A dog is a good companion."

I guessed he was talking about Jet. "Yes, she seems a sweet wee thing. But I don't want to get my hopes up." At that point, the organ began to play something slow and serious, and Craig squeezed my fingers briefly, then faced front.

A door at the side opened with a creak, and the minister shuffled in. He stopped and bowed his head as he passed Hamish's polished oak coffin, which had a commanding position in the middle of the transept. With the halting gait of someone suffering from arthritis, the reverend slowly ascended the few steps to his stone pulpit, and then the service began.

The funeral went about as well as could be expected. Mrs Douglas sat stiffly at the front, clutching a handkerchief and accompanied by her daughter. On her other side was a young family that, Craig informed me, belonged to her son. Hymns were sung, prayers were said, and the eulogy was... appropriate.

Unfortunately it didn't tell me anything I hadn't already uncovered about Hamish. As we filed out after the service was finished, I suppressed a sigh. Maybe I could talk to his family afterwards. Or, better still, get Trinity chatting with them.

She, however, was doing a meerkat impersonation. "Is that Richard?" she asked, craning her neck and motioning at a dark-suited figure near the back of the church.

Being taller, I could see better over the departing congregation. "I think so," I muttered back. Interestingly, the farrier was accompanied by the sergeant major, the one he'd met with at the pub who Craig had said was the local vet.

"'Scuse me then. I'm gonna go have a chat with him." Weaving her way through the crowd, she disappeared in their direction.

Beside me, Craig made a face. "What?" I asked.

He pressed his lips together. "Not here. I'll tell you later."

After the short grave-side ceremony, people headed for their cars to drive the short distance to The Queen's Arms, where afternoon tea was to be served in Hamish's memory.

But before I had even had a chance to offer Craig a lift, a man in a dark suit hurried up to us. He addressed my employer. "Lady Letham, Her Majesty requests a word with you." Behind him, I could see Queen Elizabeth bearing down on us.

"Of course, young man." Lady L tucked the order of service into her handbag and adjusted her gloves. The smile that creased her face when her old friend reached us was genuine. But she knew better than to speak first.

"Alice." The queen's voice was as distinct in real-life as it was on the television. "How have you been?" She held out a black-gloved hand.

Lady L took her hand and bobbed her head. "I must apologise, my dear Libby, my ankle is quite useless these days, and I am no longer able to curtsey. But I am keeping fine, thank you. How is dear Philip?"

The queen paused for a second before replying. "He is living quietly. We do jigsaws together at the weekends." I remembered hearing on the news that Prince Philip had stepped back from public duties.

Then the Queen turned to Craig. "Mr MacDonald, I believe you are to be in charge of the stud now that Mr Douglas is gone?"

Craig gave her a neck bow. "Aye, Your Majesty. Thank you for the honour."

She pressed her lips together. "The stallion, Lochnagar Golden Eagle. I believe he was the one who attacked Mr Douglas?"

Now it was Craig's turn to pause before replying. "Mr Douglas was found in Eagle's box, aye. But we don't know exactly what happened."

"Nevertheless, I cannot afford to have a dangerous horse as part of my breeding programme. Please make arrangements with the vets forthwith. I shall make enquiries with other studs about purchasing a replacement stallion."

Craig's face blanched as he realised what she was saying. He opened his mouth as if to argue with her, but before he could commit a huge faux pas with his employer, Lady Letham interrupted.

"Libby, dear, have you met Ms Paterson, my horse trainer?" She gestured at me.

Startled, I bobbed a curtsey at the Queen, got my legs in a tangle and nearly fell over. Cheeks flaming, I dared to glance at the monarch as I straightened up. She looked bemused.

"If I may make a suggestion," Lady Letham continued, one pencilled eyebrow raised questioningly, "perhaps you might send the horse to Isobel instead, and see if she can retrain him. After all, I understand that the police haven't yet completed their investigations. We may find that the poor beast is quite innocent in all of this."

The queen looked me up and down, as if trying to decide if I was up to the job. "What qualifications do you have?"

"I'm certified as an Advanced Horsemanship Trainer. I worked my way through Pony Club exams as a kid. And I ride dressage at Elementary, hoping to step up to Medium soon." I caught Craig glancing sideways at me as I reeled off my horsey CV.

"You know that I get all my horses started using Monty Roberts' methods?" Her head tilted slightly.

"I'd heard that, yes, Your Majesty. I admire his techniques."

She glanced at Lady Letham, then back at me. Her chin jerked up. "Two weeks," she stated. "If there is no improvement in his behaviour within that time, then call the vets.

Meantime, arrange with Mr MacDonald for his delivery, and payment of your fees."

I had to work hard to stop my jaw from dropping. The queen would *pay* me to train Eagle? I'd happily have done it for nothing, just for the chance to save the horse. But I knew better than to argue with her. "Thank you, ma'am."

One of the dark-suited men cleared his throat politely. "Ma'am, if I may interrupt? The helicopter will be waiting."

The queen nodded, then turned to my employer. "Alice, do come and take tea when we are back at Balmoral in the summer. I would stay longer, but sadly we have to return to London now, it being garden party season."

"I would be honoured." Lady Letham bobbed her head again.

With that, the Queen and her party were gone.

"Thank you," I said to Lady Letham. "Thank you *so* much for suggesting I take Eagle. I couldn't bear it if he was..." I trailed off. It was something every animal owner had to face at some point, but for a young, fit horse it just seemed wrong.

"I could see that in your face, my dear." She turned to Craig. "And in yours. I think you might have found yourself looking for a new job, had I not intervened."

He ducked his head. "Aye. Thank you."

Lady Letham clapped her hands. "Now, what's this I hear about tea and scones?"

———

THE FUNCTION ROOM of The Queen's Arms had less tartan decoration than the public bar. But only by a hair's breadth. However, there were so many people in the large room that it was difficult to see much of anything at all.

No sooner had we arrived than Lady L collared a waitress and got a special delivery of tea and scones to one of the small tables dotted around the outside of the room. One hand propped on her walking stick, the other elegantly sipping from a china cup, she sat and held court. I hadn't realised how popular she was in the area, but she had a regular stream of people dropping past to say hello or pass the time of day.

In another corner, Trinity was surrounded by a group of men, including the sergeant major and the lonesome cowboy. She looked like she was keeping them all entertained, and I hoped she'd have some interesting gossip for me later.

"What were you going to tell me earlier?" I asked Craig, nodding in their direction.

He followed my gaze, then checked over his shoulder to make sure nobody was listening. "It might be nothing, but—"

"Craig MacDonald! Congratulations to you!" A loud-voiced man in a tweed jacket appeared from nowhere and interrupted us, clapping Craig on the back so hard I saw him wince. "Stud Manager to the Queen, eh? There'll be no stopping you now." Then he noticed me. "Is this your new girl? Got another one on the go so soon?"

"This is my friend, Izzy Paterson. She's horse trainer to Lady Letham," Craig said firmly, then gave me a quick sideways glance. "Izzy has just secured Her Majesty as a client, she's going to train one of her horses. Izzy, this is Pat McDade, who runs the local agricultural feed stores."

My ears had locked on to Craig's use of the word 'friend', but I tried not to react. Perhaps he was as confused as I was about what was going on between us? But Pat's comment about him having 'another one on the go' gave me a queasy feeling in my gut. "Oh yes, I've seen McDades stores." I held out my hand. "Nice to meet you, Mr McDade."

"Please, call me Pat." Behind him was a wispy woman in a purple patterned dress. He ushered her forward. "Francine, come and meet the Queen's horse trainer. Izzy, wasn't it?"

"Lovely to make your acquaintance," Francine gushed, grasping my hand in a surprisingly strong grip for such a thin woman. "You're training Her Majesty's horses?"

"Horse," I corrected her. "She's sending her stallion to me for some... remedial training."

"How wonderful!" Her eyes lit up with excitement, then she clasped my arm. "Tell me, do you have any availability right now? My show jumper has been a bit of a handful lately. Some training is probably just what he needs."

"Um, yes, I think so." This was all happening rather quickly, and my brain was struggling to keep up. Perhaps I should've asked the server for coffee, rather than tea. "We could probably squeeze him in."

"Perfect!" She turned to her husband. "Darling, could we send Darcy over to Glengowrie tomorrow? Can you drive the lorry for me?"

Holding up a hand, I cleared my throat. "Monday would be better. Give us a chance to catch up, since we've been away all day today." It would also give me time to prepare for the two new horses.

"Monday it is then." Pat nodded in satisfaction. "We'll get to you about ten."

I blinked several times. It seemed like my training calendar for the next few weeks had been organised for me, without me lifting a finger.

"Now, Craig," Pat put an arm around Craig's shoulders and led him off in the direction of Trinity's group, "have you considered joining us? We have a space, now that Hamish is gone..."

That was all I heard as they disappeared into the crowd, but the whole encounter left me reeling. Within the space of an hour I'd secured my first two training clients, discovered that my maybe-boyfriend was possibly a serial philanderer and thought of me just as a friend, and, to top it off, it looked like he was about to be recruited into a secret horseman's organisation.

Today was just getting weirder and weirder...

———

THINGS TOOK an even stranger turn just a minute or two later. Standing with my back to the wall and my teacup clasped in front of me like an invisible barrier, I was trying to decide whether to join Lady L, or continue people-watching in introverted isolation.

I was quite comfortable on my own, and approaching strangers to make idle chit-chat had never been my strong suit, so I was leaning towards the interested onlooker option, when, all of a sudden, winter arrived...

"Good afternoon, Ms Paterson," said a dark voice to my right.

I spun round in alarm, almost upsetting my cup of tea in the process. "Oh! It's you!"

Warm brown eyes met mine. *Sergeant Lovell,* possibly the last person I'd expected to see here. But then I remembered something from the crime dramas I liked to watch. "Are you here to see if the murderer has come to gloat?" I asked, surreptitiously placing my napkin on the saucer under my cup to soak up the spill.

The side of his mouth quirked up. "Something like that."

Then I realised the flaw in my argument. "But, wait—I thought the police had decided Hamish's death was just an accident?"

He pointed to my cup. "Can I get you another?"

I blinked. Okay, he wasn't going to answer my question. "Um, I'm fine, thanks. I have to drive back soon and we'll never get there if I have to make hundreds of pit stops."

He laughed at that, showing almost-perfect, almost-white

teeth. It was then that I noticed he was in civvies, not uniform.

"Plain clothes?" I asked, indicating his dark grey suit and pointy black shoes.

"That's for detectives." He shrugged. "I'm on a day off. Came to pay my respects." His lips twitched again. "And keep an eye open for murderers."

Surely that was an invitation to enquire further? I tried again to get an answer. "Any luck so far?"

This time it was an eyebrow that twitched. "Well, a casual observer might wonder if there was more than one suspect in this room. But of course, in an official capacity, I couldn't possibly make any such observation."

I swallowed, realising that I was most probably one of those suspects. "So you don't think it's accidental death?"

He looked steadily at me for what felt like a full minute but must only have been seconds. But it was long enough for heat to grow under my collar. I resisted the temptation to loosen a button. Or three.

"You said, 'we'?" he said, eventually. On seeing my puzzled look, he clarified his question. "You said 'we' were driving back?"

"Oh! I drove Lady Letham here, since she can't drive any longer because of her ankle. And my flatmate, Trinity, came too." I jerked my chin at the corner where Trinity was still holding court.

He nodded. "So when do you expect to arrive back at Glengowrie?"

I checked my watch. "Probably around six. Then we have the evening checks to do on the horses."

"Does that mean you might be free about seven thirty?" He swallowed, his next words coming in a bit of a rush. "Could I take you for some dinner?" He must've seen my jaw drop. "I have a... business proposition for you," he added.

Over in the corner, my *friend* Craig was laughing uproari-
ously at something Pat McDade had said. I met Sergeant
Lovell's eyes. "Only if you'll tell me one thing?"

"I will if I can."

"What's your first name?"

CHAPTER FOURTEEN

SERGEANT LOVELL, it turned out, was called Dean, and, out of uniform and out of his 'patch' he loosened up considerably, and became quite good company.

The family-run Italian restaurant he'd chosen was in nearby Blairgowrie, since Glengowrie was still flooded. With arched openings reminiscent of a wine cellar, whitewashed walls, and candles on every table, it felt comfortable and friendly.

Once we'd eaten and moved on to the more formal part of the evening, Dean leaned forward and put his elbows on the table.

It transpired that the 'business proposition' he had for me was to investigate Hamish's financial dealings. Somehow or other—I guess that's what policemen do—he'd discovered that I had some experience as a computer hacker.

"More wine for the pretty lady?" The waiter hovered at my elbow, green bottle in his hand.

Since his last visit, my glass had somehow managed to empty itself. "Just a little," I said. He proceeded to fill it again, before I stopped him, putting my hand over the top of the glass. "I have to get up early in the morning," I explained.

Once the waiter had gone, I focussed on the policeman again. "So you think he might have been involved in something that got him killed?"

"It's possible."

"But what about the spider bite?"

"That's where my theory falls down. Accidental death fits with the facts."

"So why do you want me to check him out?"

He swirled the water in his glass, watching the lights dance and sparkle through the facets of crystal. "It just... doesn't *feel* right. The man wasn't popular—apart from with his cronies at the horseman's club."

"You know about that?"

He gave me a look from under those dark eyelashes. "I'm a policeman, remember?"

I raised a hand. "Sorry."

"But wait—how did *you* know about that?"

It was hard to suppress the smile. "I'm a computer hacker, remember?"

He clinked his glass on mine. "Touché." Then his brow furrowed. "Does that mean *you* were checking up on him?"

"No flies on you, copper." I took a swig of wine, remembering the dark shapes in Eagle's vision. "His death just didn't seem like an accident." Then something occurred to me. "Am I right that the vet has taken over for him in the guild? He was the deputy, wasn't he?"

"Yes. Oliver Seaforth."

The sergeant major was definitely taller and wider than Hamish, like the man in the pictures the stallion had shown to me. "Do you know if he ever wears a hat? One with a brim?"

Dean's head tilted. "Maybe." He lifted his hands. "I don't know. Why d'you ask?"

I shook my head. "Nothing. But would becoming a grand master or whatever they call it be enough motive for murder?"

"Probably not." He narrowed his eyes. "Getting Hamish's job at the Queen's stud might be a better motive."

"You mean Craig? I talked to him. He doesn't seem bothered about the promotion. And he already earns more than he spends, from what he told me, so money isn't a motive."

Dean didn't look convinced, but with a jerk of his chin he seemed to dismiss that topic of conversation. "That's why I want to check his financial dealings. Rule out gambling debts or similar as a reason, in case he got himself into trouble with the local ne'er-do-wells."

"Are your bosses okay with you keeping the case open, if they think it's accidental death?"

He ducked his head and started rearranging the salt and pepper cellars in front of his place setting.

Like a guilty schoolboy. "They don't know?"

He glanced up at me. "I'm hoping it might stand me in good stead in my application for detective rank."

I took another swig of my wine. "So why are they paying my investigation fee?"

This time the flower vase got added into the mix. He studiously avoided my eyes.

"They're not?" I moved the pepper grinder out of the way to get his attention.

With a sigh, he sat back in his chair. "I'll pay. It'll be worth it if it helps get me to DS."

"Detective Sergeant?"

He nodded.

"D'you not have to do an exam for that?"

"Yes, but there are only so many spots here in the Highlands. So if I don't want to end up in a big city station, it would help my application to solve a case like this."

"Still, you shouldn't have to go paying out of your own pocket. How about I don't invoice till you've solved the case, and then the bigwigs will maybe pay my bill out of gratitude to you?"

"Would you do that? Do you not work on a retainer?"

I pursed my lips. "Can I be honest with you?"

His eyebrows crept upwards, then he moved a hand up and down, obviously alluding to the uniform he wasn't wearing. "Policeman, remember? Honesty is always the best policy!"

"Of course." I felt my cheeks going pink. "It's just—my business is pretty new. I've only had a few proper clients so far, plus I solved an embezzlement case at my work in London. Helped solve," I clarified. "My colleague, Dev, worked with me on it. He'll work with me sometimes in Aye Spy—he's actually better with the financial stuff, so I might pass this on to him."

"I spy?"

"Aye Spy Investigations. My business. Well, my IT security business. There's my horse training business too." I passed a card across the table.

His forehead puckered. "I thought you worked for Lady Letham?"

"I do. But as part of the deal she lets me use three of the stables for external clients. It doesn't take me all day to do her horses."

"So," he ticked off on his fingers, "you have a job training horses, a second job training horses and a third one doing computer consulting. Did I get that right?"

"Yeah." I didn't mention to him that I was also hoping to get some clients who would pay me to compete their horses for them. Once my name got around a bit more, of course. I wasn't exactly beating them off with a stick right now.

He shook his head. "No wonder you never get any time off."

"Talking of which," I consulted my watch, "I should really get back, if you don't mind. I usually check the horses each night at bed-time. Thank you for a lovely dinner, and I'll see what we can find out for you about Hamish."

Pushing his chair away from the table, he stood up. "Let me just pay the bill, then I'll drive you back."

A couple of minutes later, we were out in the quiet street, a dog barking somewhere in the distance, and the faint smell of garlic emanating from the kitchens behind the restaurant. Dean had parked at the other side of the road, and as I stepped off the kerb, somehow I lost my footing and stumbled.

Before I hit the tarmac, a strong hand grabbed my arm and swung me back to my feet—where I collided with Dean's chest. His very hard, very manly chest.

It was like the earth stopped turning for a couple of seconds, my gaze trapped in his, my body held close against him.

Feather-light, he dropped a kiss on my lips. "Too much wine for you this evening, my lady." Taking my elbow, he turned me carefully and escorted me to the passenger side of his car.

We didn't talk on the way home. I spent most of the time staring out of the window, chastising myself for letting him kiss me when I was—well, what *was* I to Craig? His *friend*, he'd said, just that afternoon. Was that really all I was to him?

I looked at Dean's profile, shadowy in the dark. Despite the evening we'd spent together, I knew very little about him —his conversation had been about current events, or funny stories from the local community. Nothing about himself. He was the classic tall, dark stranger.

Anyway, like he'd pointed out, did I really have time to be seeing anyone right now? I had two businesses I was trying to establish, plus a new boss to impress.

Lifting my chin, I watched the moonlit landscape flit by as we drew closer to Glengowrie. It had a soporific effect, and I was feeling quite sleepy when Dean finally parked his car under the old oak tree.

He ran round to open the door for me, then took my arm as I turned toward the stable yard. "I'll chum you while you check the horses. Can't have you falling over again and breaking your neck."

"Thanks," I mumbled through a yawn. Between tiredness and wine, I was having difficulty making my legs do their job properly, and his support was quite helpful. Not to mention that he smelled deliciously of cocoa butter. Or did he just remind me of chocolate, with his dark looks and brown eyes?

We were greeted by a few suspicious snorts, and some ticklish whiskers as we progressed around the yard, but fortunately there were no sickly horses, and nobody lying too close to a corner of their stable and unable to get up. All was well.

Dean stopped with me at the door to the cottage. "I know it was really a work thing, but... tonight's been good. Thanks, Izzy."

My head spun at his proximity. It was like I'd stepped into a chocolatier, surrounded by the most intoxicating smells. And then I was surrounded by his arms, and his lips met mine.

For a minute, I felt like Charlie in the chocolate factory, living the dream. I swear the policeman even *tasted* of chocolate, however that was possible.

With a last peck on the nose, he released me, and opened

the door behind me. "Till next time," he said with a flicker of a smile, and disappeared into the night.

———

THE NEXT MORNING, Trinity came down the stairs to find me sitting at the breakfast table in something of a daze, staring at the list of ingredients on the cornflakes pack as if they were written in Swahili. "Did someone stay out a bit late last night?"

"Mmm," I mumbled.

She gave me a blackbird look, all sharp eyes and tilted head. "This calls for a Kalista special." Grabbing her keys from the shelf beside the door, she beckoned me forwards. "C'mon. I'll take you. The horses can wait for ten minutes. And ain't you lucky the café missed getting flooded."

A minute later, I was slumped in the passenger seat of her Mini and we were zooming out of the yard.

"So, tell me, what's the story from last night?"

"Um," I scrunched my eyes. It was too bright today. Scrabbling in her glove box, I managed to find a pair of sunglasses and slipped them on. "Dean wants me to do a bit of investigation for him. Check out Hamish's finances."

"Dean?" I didn't need to look at her to know that her eyebrows had rocketed.

"Sergeant Lovell."

"First-name terms!" She glanced sideways at me. "And...?"

I put my head in my hands, as memories flooded back. "And he kissed me."

She banged the heel of her hand against the steering wheel. "I knew it! He likes you."

"I'd had a bit much wine—"

"Never!" she interrupted, sarcastically.

My eyes would have rolled harder if my head hadn't hurt.

"—and I stumbled. He caught me before I fell. And the kiss just, kind of, happened. It was like a brotherly thing." Then I remembered that he'd kissed me again at the cottage door. "I think," I added.

That earned me another sideways look. "We can re-visit that later." The car slowed. "But that's us here." She parked at the kerb outside the shop and jerked her thumb at the door. "Let's get you some caffeine."

The bell over the door tinkled as we entered the café, and I dropped the sunglasses back over my eyes, because it was almost as bright inside as outside.

Scarlet curtains hung at the windows, with the lower half covered by white nets hanging from a brass pole. Ladder-backed chairs with crimson cushions surrounded tables covered in strawberry-patterned cotton tablecloths. And everything was brightly lit by hanging lights with red vinyl shades. It seemed like Kalista's favourite colour was red. Or perhaps she just wanted to give the place a warm and cozy feel?

Trinity approached the counter and ordered my drink for me.

While she did that, I noticed that the Large sisters were back at their window table again. "...and she was seen having dinner with that policeman, the one who jolted Zoe Wainwright, at the Aye-talian in Blairgowrie," the larger Miss Large was saying.

"Jilted her, aye," her thinner sibling said.

"And," Edie leaned conspiratorially across the table, "they were seen kissing!"

"No, they never did?"

It was only then that I realised they were probably talking about me and Dean. I buried my chin in my collar and turned my back on them, sure my cheeks were flaming red.

"Only been here five minutes and she's already sunk her claws into the most illegible bachelor in the area."

"Aye, eligible bachelor, aye."

"Here." Trinity thrust a large cup of cappuccino at me, then glanced over at the window table. "Let's get out of here."

"Thanks," I grunted, as we both hurried out of the café.

With a groan, I sank into the seat of her car. "How did word get out so quickly? We weren't even here, we were in Blairgowrie."

Trinity shrugged, then put the car into gear. "Small towns, nothing better to do than talk about your neighbours." She cut her eyes at me. "An' they told me before I came up here that I'd find village life boring."

"Well, they need to find something else to talk about." I gave her a sideways look, the caffeine beginning to do its thing on my neural pathways. "Talking of gossip, you never told me how you got on at the funeral?"

"It was a sad day," she said with a smirk.

"And the farrier...?"

Hurtling round the corner of the stable yard, she screeched to a stop outside the cottage. "We're here. Get that coffee down you, girl. We've got work to do."

"And the farrier?" I persisted. "C'mon. I spilled my beans." That sounded weird. "So to speak."

A smug expression crossed her face. "Got a date with him on Saturday."

I raised the cup at her, then took a slug. "Good on ya!" The caffeine hit my system like an electric shock zapping a cartoon character, and my eyes pinged fully open.

Stepping out of the car, she made a 'hurry up' motion at me. "C'mon. We need to get going. Eagle arrives today, remember?"

The thought of seeing Slytherin Stan again made me shudder. "Ugh." Depositing the sunglasses, I clambered out.

She looked back at me. "We need to have a catch up. I've loads more to tell you from the funeral, but we ain't had a minute since then. Maybe when we get Eagle sorted?" She strode off without waiting for a reply.

Intrigued, I stared at the spot where she'd been standing just a few seconds ago. *Wonder what she found out?* Cradling the coffee, I hurried after her. Maybe the yard work would finish the job the cappuccino had started and clear the fog in my brain.

But the thing that woke me up properly wasn't my work. Instead, I was catapulted into the day by the sight that greeted me when the Balmoral lorry pulled up in the yard a while later. Driving the truck wasn't Stan the groom, as I'd expected. It was Craig.

My cheeks coloured as he stepped down from the cab and raised a hand.

"Over here." I motioned to the box we'd allocated to the stallion, hoping Craig was far enough away not to wonder at my blush.

He nodded and started to open the ramp to get the horse out.

Unlatching the half-door, I held it wide while he led the stallion in.

"Let me just get his saddle and bridle from the lorry," Craig said as he came out, giving me a quick peck on the cheek as he passed.

Convinced I was turning pink again, I watched in confusion as he retrieved the tack from the lorry, then marched off towards the tack room. Then my brow puckered, and I hurried after him.

"I've just put them on this empty peg," he said as I almost fell through the door. "Unless there's anywhere special you want them?"

I ignored his question and asked one of my own instead. "How did you know where the tack room was?"

"I was shown it at…" he trailed off, looking guilty.

"At…?"

With a sigh, he sat down at the table. "At my interview."

"Your interview?" I repeated stupidly, dropping into the chair beside him before my knees gave way.

Picking at some dry skin beside his thumbnail, he kept his eyes fixed on his hands. "I interviewed for your job. Unsuccessfully, obviously." He risked a glance at me. "You were the better candidate."

My mind whirled. "So that was why Lady Letham knew you at the funeral?"

"Aye."

I leaned back in my chair, wishing I hadn't finished my cappuccino. News like this *definitely* needed coffee to help it make sense. "Why didn't you tell me before?"

He shrugged. "It never came up. And I could see as soon as I met you that you were a shoo-in for the job. It was always a bit of a reach for me."

There was silence for a moment as my befuddled mind tried to process this new information. Then I heard Trinity's voice from outside. "She's in there. In the tack room."

Footsteps crunched across the yard, and then Sergeant Lovell appeared in the doorway. He looked from Craig to me, and a muscle tightened in his jaw. "Good morning Ms Paterson, Mr MacDonald."

"Hi," I said, giving him a feeble wave. For the first time in my life I wished I was one of those girls who didn't leave the house without her 'face' on. My cheeks were surely puce by now, a colour that would only be concealed by the thickest of makeup. I pointed at the chair opposite. "Take a seat."

"It's okay, I'll stand," he said stiffly, taking off his peaked cap and tucking it under his arm. "I just came to see if you'd heard the news?"

I looked at him blankly. "News?"

Beside me, Craig shook his head. "What's happened?"

Dean's eyes fixed on Craig. "Oliver Seaforth has been found dead."

My hand shot to my mouth. "Really? How? When?"

At the same time, Craig said, "But I was just speaking to him yesterday."

"Yes." The sergeant's voice was laced with suspicion. "And now he turns up dead."

Craig's mouth fell open. "Ye canna think I would do such a thing? I hardly knew the man. And why on earth would I kill him?"

The policeman raised an eyebrow. "When two prominent members of the same society are killed, we start to wonder if there's a connection. Maybe the books were getting cooked and those two got wind of it. Maybe someone wanted to become a member and their face didn't fit. Or maybe some-one," at this point he gave Craig a hard stare, "wanted a promotion."

"Dean, you can't go just accusing people like that without some evidence," I interjected.

"Dean?" Craig turned to me, hurt showing in his green eyes.

Rats. "I, um—"

"Perhaps you could give us a minute, Mr MacDonald?" the policeman interrupted. "I need to ask Ms Paterson some questions."

His jaw clenched, Craig pushed his chair back. "I'll just go and get Eagle settled."

We waited in silence until we heard the rumble of Craig's voice and the tinkle of Trinity's from the other side of the yard.

Dean took the chair opposite me, put his hat on the table and steepled his hands. "Mr MacDonald is here rather early?"

I checked my watch reflexively. *Ten o'clock.* Why had life got so complicated before I'd even had my second coffee of the day? "He's delivering the Queen's stallion to me for training. He just arrived. Coffee?" I asked, getting up and going over to the kettle.

"Tea, please. Milk and two."

I busied myself making our drinks.

"So you can't give him an alibi for last night?"

I swung round, almost throwing hot water over the copper in the process. "How could you think that? *You* were the last person I saw last evening. It's well over an hour's drive from Balmoral in a lorry, and Craig just got here. He must've left before nine. Ask Trinity if you don't believe me."

He came over and took the mugs from me, setting them on the counter. Then he put his hands on my forearms. "I'm sorry. I shouldn't have said that. You just—" he glanced down, "—I mean, I shouldn't have jumped to conclusions. Sorry."

Not trusting myself to speak, I nodded. It *sounded* like he was a little jealous of Craig. But why would he be? It was very confusing. *Men* were very confusing. I'd have to tell Trinity later and see what she thought, since she had better instincts with people.

"Okay." Letting go of my arms, he picked up his cup and spooned sugar into it, then sat back down at the table. "I've got something to ask you. Two things, actually."

Grabbing my coffee, I sat down heavily. "Yes?"

"Firstly, the investigation into Hamish's death has been re-opened—this new development is just too coincidental. So my bosses have agreed to pay your fees, and we'd like you to investigate Mr Seaforth as well. They say they'll raise a purchase order."

"Oh-kay," I said slowly, unsurprised at the police bureaucracy after my time spent working for a large organisation in London. I sipped at my drink. "I'll see what I can do."

"And secondly," he continued, then picked up a teaspoon and started stirring his tea.

"Secondly?" I prompted, wondering what was coming next.

Brown eyes met mine. "Would you consider coming out with me again this weekend? We could go to the cinema in Dundee. Or ten-pin bowling. Or we could do dinner," a slow smile lit up his face, "but avoid the wine this time."

I almost laughed at that. However, I wasn't ready to commit to a date. I was too confused about my feelings for him and Craig. "Let me see how today goes, and I'll let you know. But first, tell me more about how Mr Seaforth died?"

―――――

THE VET, it turned out, had been found dead on the floor of his surgery when his cleaner had turned up for work early that morning. An empty syringe lay beside him, and it looked as if he'd been injected with an overdose of animal anaesthetic.

"We might have thought suicide," Dean explained, "except that we found the needle mark on the back of his right arm. Not the sort of place you'd inject yourself. And anyway, he was right-handed."

"So we're possibly looking at someone from the Horse-man's Guild as a suspect?"

"*We* are. *You* just need to concentrate on their financial dealings. See if you can find any crossover, or anything suspicious. I was just explaining the context so you understand what we're thinking." He picked up his cap and stepped towards the door. "Now, I need to take Mr MacDonald in for questioning."

"Questioning?" I followed him out into the yard, where Craig and Trinity were talking outside Eagle's box.

Dean acted like he hadn't heard me, pulled Craig aside, and spoke urgently to him.

Craig's face fell, and he nodded briefly. Then he strode towards me. "I have tae go back. Will ye be able to pick up Daisy and Allegra this week? There's only two spaces in the wee lorry so I couldnae bring them wi' me today, I'm sorry."

His accent was definitely stronger than usual. I remembered it had been that way at the pub, after a few beers. But did stress or anxiety maybe make it stronger too? I didn't know him well enough to be sure, but it seemed possible. Being interviewed for a second time by the police would be enough to worry most people.

"I could try to come up tomorrow?" I suggested. "Probably the afternoon, once we've got the horses done here."

"Aye, that should be fine. Give me a ring before you leave, so I know when to expect you." He leaned slightly towards me, as if he was going to kiss my cheek, then seemed to think better of it. Instead, he clasped my arm. "I'll be seeing you. Soon, I hope." With a quick smile that didn't reach his eyes, he stepped into the cab of the lorry and drove off.

Dean jumped into his police car and followed after Craig, raising his hand in farewell as he passed me.

The two vehicles disappeared in a cloud of dust, and Trinity appeared at my side. "What were all that about?"

I sighed. "The vet, Oliver Seaforth, has been found dead, and the police want to question Craig."

"That's so not right! He wouldn't ever do something like that..." She paused, staring at the cloud of dust, then frowned at me. "Would he?"

"I'M GIVING UP ON MEN," I announced as we congregated in the tack room for lunch. Even though Stables Cottage was only a few steps away, there was something satisfying about keeping work separate from our home life, and eating 'on the hoof' as it were.

"What's brought that on?" Trinity picked up a cracker and started spreading butter on it.

In the corner, Jorja curled up on the old saddle pad we'd placed there especially for her, and soon was snoring contentedly.

"You heard what those gossips at the café said about Dean —that he jilted some woman. And Pat McDade said something about Craig having 'another girl on the go so soon'. Plus, Craig introduced me yesterday as his 'friend'." I picked up an apple and started to slice it. "I really thought we were a bit more than friends."

"Maybe it's time to have 'the talk' with him?"

"The talk?"

"The state of the union. Are we just friends, or more? Is this just dating, or are we exclusive... You get the picture?"

I nodded. "But if he's a bit of a philanderer like Mr McDade said, I'm not interested. There were enough players in London. I don't need the drama."

She waved a tomato in the air, before taking a bite of it. "So this is an example of why we need to cultivate the local gossips. To find out what *really* happened."

"But is gossip not, by its very nature, mostly untrue?"

"You know what they say. There ain't no smoke without fire. But you need enough sources to get the full picture. Like, from all angles. One swallow does not make a summer, and all that."

I sighed. This was *so* not my area of expertise. "Any chance you could check out the gossip for me? About both of them? Dean has asked me out again, and I don't know whether to go."

"You absolutely should," she mumbled through a mouthful of cheese and biscuits. "You could do with getting out a bit more, spending less time on that computer. And he's hot."

"Yeah, but being hot isn't everything."

"Is for me."

That comment totally deserved an eye roll. "What about—"

I was interrupted by a knock on the door. "Hello?" said a male voice

From the corner, Jorja barked, then her nails clicked across the wooden floor, her tail wagging slightly as the door creaked open.

A full black beard and large horn-rimmed glasses peered around the jamb. "I thought I heard voices. May I come in?"

"Um, yes, I suppose so."

The stranger entered the room. Wearing a red check shirt, jeans and a grey cardigan, he had almost as much hair on his head as in his beard, so it was hard to see his face, as if he was hiding from the world. He looked at Trinity, then swallowed. "I—I'm looking for Isobel Paterson," he said, his eyes never leaving her face.

She jerked her chin in my direction. "Wrong girl, mate. I'm Trinity."

His adam's apple bobbled. "Hello, Trinity, nice to meet you. I'm Neil Etherington from the Gowrie Gazette." Then he turned to me. "Ms Paterson," he extended a hand, "We heard you were working for Lady Letham, and that you were a witness to the recent murder at Balmoral. I wonder if you might spare me a few minutes for an interview?"

"Oh, I don't think your readers would be—"

"What she's trying to say, mate," interrupted Trinity, "is

that she'd be happy to speak to you as long as you'll include a link to the website for her horse training business."

The boy reporter was staring at Trinity again, his mouth hanging slightly open. I couldn't decide whether he was entranced by her, or had such a sheltered upbringing that he wasn't used to seeing women who looked like her.

With a slight shake of his head, he seemed to remember why he was here. "Th—That would be beautiful, I mean, wonderful."

His slip-up answered the entranced versus sheltered question for me—obviously he was appreciative of her feminine charms. Unfortunately for him, I didn't get any corresponding vibes from her. I sighed. "We can speak in here, if that suits?" I waved him to a chair.

Pulling a phone out of his pocket, he pressed some buttons and then placed it on the table between us. Then spun it round the other way. "G—great. I'll just record the interview, if that's okay—"

Trinity pushed her chair back and stood up, grabbing a banana from the fruit bowl which she raised in salute. "Excuse me. I'll go check on Eagle. Leave you guys to it." Before I could protest, she disappeared out of the door.

Clark Kent spent the next twenty minutes asking me various questions about the murder and my background. I did my best not to tell him anything which would annoy the police or compromise their investigation. And any time I got twitchy about the personal questions, I reminded myself that it would be good publicity for my training business. Despite his seeming shyness, he was good at his job, and actually made me feel somewhat at ease.

When his questions dried up, he motioned outside. "Would it be possible to get a photo of you, maybe with one of the horses?"

My initial instinct was to say no, but then I remembered that this was like free advertising for us. "Um, okay."

Trinity was sweeping the yard when we went outside, but she stopped when she saw us.

"He wants a photo," I said, then scanned the boxes. With a sinking heart, I realised that Eagle was the only horse that was in just now; the rest were out grazing in their various fields. Would the Queen mind if I was photographed with her prize stallion? Even if he *was* somewhat disgraced right now?

"Eagle is a client's horse," I said, leading the reporter over to the stallion's box. "Would you be able to do something artistic so he's not too recognisable?

"I'm sure I could. If you stand there," he pointed, then glanced upwards to check the position of the sun and moved a couple of steps sideways before crouching down with his phone, "I'll get an interesting angle from here."

"I thought reporters usually had photographers in tow?" Trinity moved a little closer. "Union rights or whatever."

He shrugged. "W—we're just a little paper. We all have to muck in." Taking one more shot, he stood and addressed Trinity. "Is it you who's starting the dancing classes I heard about?"

"Good to hear the jungle drums are getting the word out," she said with a grin, brushing a stalk of straw from her t-shirt. "Yeah, that's me. Horse groom by day, salsa dancer by night."

"P—perhaps I could do a piece on you for next week's paper?"

"Sure thing. D'you want to do it now?"

Checking the time on his phone, he grimaced. "I'm afraid I'll need to get this one written up to make our copy deadline. I'll come back next week, if that's okay?"

"It's a date," she said, and then resumed her sweeping.

For a moment, I thought Neil was about to faint. I'd already taken a step towards him, ready to grab him if he collapsed, when he gave himself a little shake and stood taller. "Sorry, sugar dip," he said by way of excuse, and pointed at a bicycle propped against the oak tree. "I need to learn to eat more calories."

"Mmm," I said, but I wasn't taken in. The roving reporter had it bad for my flatmate.

I had a feeling that there was a handsome guy under all that hair, and he seemed really intelligent and personable. But hardly what you'd call 'hot'. So, from what she'd said earlier, he'd have no chance with her.

"See you next week," Neil raised a hand in farewell, then strode over to his bike, popped a helmet on his head, and set off down the drive.

Like a typical Brit, I felt sorry for the underdog, and my heart twisted a little for him. Unrequited feelings must be the worst, and it was something that I, too, knew a little about...

CHAPTER FIFTEEN

OVER DINNER THAT NIGHT—GINGER, sweet potato and coconut milk stew with lentils and kale, cooked by Trinity—I finally got to hear her gossip from the funeral.

At various times, the group of men surrounding her had included the now-deceased vet, Oliver Seaforth, Pat McDade the agricultural merchant, Richard Mortimer the farrier, the minister from Crathie church, and even Craig, once he'd left me. And it seemed the men were worse gossips than most women.

One person in the group that was new to both of us was the local 'back man'—a chiropractor for horses—who was known as 'The Terminator' because of his catch phrase: "I'll be back."

I groaned when she told me that.

"Yeah. He were a bit of a looker, though. His eyes! They was so blue, like the sea."

I rolled my eyes at her. "I thought you liked the farrier?"

Her fork paused, half-way to her mouth. "I do. But a girl has to keep her options open, don't she? Succession planning, I think they call it."

Shaking my head, I took another bite of the delicious stew. "But you're still going out with Richard on Saturday?"

"Yeah. I'm meeting 'im for a drink. But," she leaned forward, "I never told you the chat. Apparently old Hamish had an argy-bargy in the pub with one of the guys from the shooting party a couple of nights before he died. The man was 'aving a go at him because they hadn't managed to shoot any deer that day."

The vegetarian in me rejoiced at that. "I wonder if the police know?"

Trinity gave me a sly look. "If you go out with your rozzer tomorrow, you could tell him."

She had a point there. "Any other tidbits?"

"Hamish weren't having a good night, that night, 'cos when his missus came to get him later on, he were in his cups and she practically dragged him out of there by his ear."

I sat back in my chair. "So the wife might have done it after all?"

Her shoulders lifted. "Maybe. But would Grisham not want more evidence than some tittle-tattle?" she said, referring to my favourite character in the TV show, *CSI*.

"You're right," I said. "I really need to get going with my research. And contact Dev to investigate their bank accounts."

She made a shooing motion with her hand. "Off you go then. I'll wash up."

———

DEV, my ex-colleague from the bank in London, wasn't as much of an introvert as me. But he was a bigger geek, wearing superhero t-shirts like they were a uniform, and able to quote reams from every *Star Trek* episode there ever was. So I knew that instant messaging would be the best way to contact him.

Me: Hey, Dev, how's it going?

Dev: Just great! I'm having a whale of a time here. You?

Me: Good thanks, getting settled and getting to know the locals. Got my first job for Aye Spy, too, and I need your help.

Dev: ??

Me: A local guy got murdered. And then another. The police want their financial dealings investigated in case there was anything strange going on. I thought that would be a job for you.

Dev: Tell me more.

I proceeded to give him all the details I knew about Hamish and Oliver, and he said he'd get right on it, and let me know as soon as he found anything interesting.

Me: And how's it going with you and Charlie?

Dev: She got a job at a tech startup down by the docks.

Me: In Dublin?

Dev: Yeah. We're sharing a flat in the centre. Right across the street from my favourite pub :)

Yay! I punched the air, glad to hear that Charlie had finally got her man.

Me: Handy. You can stagger home.

Dev: Just have to watch out for kamikaze taxis when I'm crossing the road.

Me: Lol.

Dev: Right. I'd better get started on those investigations for you so I can get you some answers.

Me: Okay. Thanks. I've got some work to do too.
   Speak soon.
Dev: Live long and prosper.

I laughed as I shut down the chat window and opened Gremlin. Dev always had good banter.

Then I paused, my fingers hovering over the keyboard. What was I going to search for? "Trin, did you hear what the name was of the guy who was arguing with Hamish?"

"Don't think they mentioned it." She opened a cupboard door and tidied away a casserole dish. "Perhaps Craig would know?"

"Mmmm."

She gave me a sharp look. "An' you could have that talk with him."

My insides knotted up. "Not sure I'm ready for that, yet."

"Yeah, but don't you think you'd better check before you go out with the policeman again? If Craig thinks you're exclusive," she made air quotes around the word, "he'll be well annoyed if he finds out you've been out with another man."

She had a point. "Oh-kay." *Oh boy.* I *so* didn't want to do this. My brain was all about the logic. And emotions just weren't logical, so I tried not to do them.

But his phone rang out. I didn't know whether to be relieved or worried. Were the police still questioning him this late in the day? I decided to send a text instead:

Me: Hey, Craig, hope all is okay. Can you give me a
   phone when you get this? Thanks, Izzy x

I debated long and hard about whether to type a kiss or not. But, up till now, we'd always signed off with an x, so it made sense to stick with it so he wouldn't think something was up. I made a face. Did men even notice such things?

While I waited for him to reply, I sent Gremlin off to search for meeting notes or minutes from the horseman's guild, to see if there were any hints of trouble or animosity.

Trinity came through from the kitchen, shooed Jorja off the armchair and plumped herself down. "So?"

"He wasn't answering. So I sent a text message."

She threw up her hands. "Technology ain't the be-all and end-all, Izzy. Like, sometimes it's best to just *talk* to people. Tell them what's in your heart."

My shoulders slumped. "That's the problem. I'm not sure I know what I feel. I mean, if I like Craig, then why did I let Dean kiss me last night?"

"Maybe you're just too polite, girl. Though he *is* a bit of a looker. But you'll work it out. When you need to. And, till then, don't be afraid to let yourself *feel* things. It ain't a crime." She picked up the TV remote control and pointed it at the screen. "Talking of which—CSI?"

———

It was almost midnight before Craig texted me back. I'd been asleep for a couple of hours, but the buzzing of my phone on the bedside table woke me up. Groggily, I felt for the lamp and switched it on, then propped myself up on an elbow and tried to focus on the phone screen.

> Craig: *Didn't want to phone in case you were asleep. It's been a difficult day. You okay?*

Collapsing back on the pillow, I groaned. The easy thing would be to pretend I hadn't seen his message till the morning, or just text back. But even I, socially inept as I often was, could tell he needed to talk. I dialled his number.

"Hey. Thanks for messaging back," I said when he answered.

"Oh, sorry, did I wake you?"

"Don't worry about it. You sounded like you could do with a chat."

I could almost hear him run a hand through his hair. "Yeah. It's been a long day."

"What happened?"

"Questions, questions, and more questions. I spent all day stuck inside in that soul-less box of a police station and it about drove me demented. They seemed to think I might have something to do with the vet's death since I obviously killed Hamish to get his job."

"But they've let you home now?"

"Only because the forensic report came back and there's no sign of me at the scene." The phone crackled as if he was changing hands. "I think they might have found some other evidence, though."

It took a minute for that to sink in. "So they may have a lead on who the real killer was?"

"Aye, or it could just be dog hairs, or from a previous client to the surgery. I suppose they'll need to rule out his customers from that day."

"True." Remembering why I'd wanted to speak to him, I changed the subject. "Craig, did you hear anything about one of the guys in the shooting party having a big argument with Hamish at the pub the night before he was killed? Something about not managing to kill any deer?"

There was a pause at the other end of the line. "I think maybe that's what they were talking about up the hill the next day. They were joshing with the guy. But it didn't sound serious."

"Do you know the man's name?"

"Torquil something. I didn't get a surname."

Would that be enough to track him down? Maybe he'd be on a Friends list on FaceBook, if I could find one of the others. "What about the others? Did you catch any of their full names?"

"There was one they called 'Slowhand'. When I asked why, they said his name was Eric Clarence. Like Eric Clapton. Hence the name."

"Thanks, that's a good lead. If you remember any of the others, you could text me."

"Will do." He yawned. "While I remember, your wee friend Trinity. Is she interested in that farrier?"

"Mmmm. She's supposed to be going out with him tomorrow."

He sucked in a breath. "Tell her to be careful. He's already been out with two or three of the lassies here on the estate, and he's left them in tears. Seems he's a bit of a lothario."

That would've been my ideal opening to ask Craig what Pat McDade had meant about him having 'another one on the go'. But I chickened out. In my defence, me being half asleep and him having had a hard day maybe wasn't the best time to tackle it. "I'll let her know. Thanks."

"Are you still coming up to get the mares tomorrow?"

"That's the plan."

"Have a coffee with me when you get there. Then we can properly catch up."

"Okay. See you tomorrow."

"Good night." He blew me a kiss, then severed the connection.

I lay back on my pillow, almost fully awake now. Was he a lothario too, or did he really like me? And who was this Torquil person? Was he the killer?

It would be hard to get to sleep again with all those questions buzzing around my brain, but the one that bothered me most of all was: what had they found at the murder scene?

I decided to text Dean, since I was awake anyway and it was possible he was too, if he'd been interviewing Craig till now.

> Me: *Hey, any more info on the vet's murder that I should know about?*

He replied pretty much straight away.

> Dean: *We found DNA evidence at the scene. But need to rule out his clients.*

Pretty much as I'd thought.

> Me: *Okay. I've got my colleague working on the financial investigations, I'm still looking at the horseman's guild angle.*
> Dean: *Let me know as soon as you find anything.*
> Me: *Will do. G'night.*

I had that dilemma about sending a kiss again, but decided against it since this was a work thing.

> Dean: *Thanks. Night.*

Good call, Izzy. But thinking about the guild made me wonder how Gremlin was getting on, and, since I was awake, I thought I might as well check.

Padding down to the lounge area as silently as I could, wrapped in a warm fleece, I sat down in front of my laptop. The blue light of the screen lit the room with a ghostly glow, augmented by the dying embers from the fire.

Suddenly, something landed beside me on the couch, and I had to stifle a scream. Then I felt stupid. *Jorja.* My hand went reflexively to my chest as my heart-rate spiked, then started to settle again as she snuggled against me.

Gremlin, it turned out, had uncovered the archive of meeting minutes from the horseman's guild. I started reading them, but of course nobody was mentioned by name again, so it was all 'member this' and 'deputy grand master that' which wasn't hugely helpful.

In the most recent meetings they had one rejected membership application, one member who had passed (and one failed) the 'Golden Horseshoe' grading, three who had attained Silver Horseshoe, and a majority of the group (but not unanimous) had agreed to pay an amount of money to a local donkey sanctuary.

None of that sounded like motive for murder, let alone double murder. *But...* I remembered the *Hamish MacBeth* audio books I used to listen to on the underground in London, where people seemed to be killed over the smallest thing. Maybe I should keep an open mind.

Closing the laptop, I gave Jorja a pat, and headed back to bed. Maybe Dev would turn up something interesting in the victims' financial records.

CHAPTER SIXTEEN

On Saturday afternoon I spent half of my journey to Balmoral deciding that I needed to get Leo entered for some local dressage competitions, so that my name would start getting recognised, and people might be interested in using me as a rider—or trainer.

The rest of the drive I spent mulling over the murder clues. It was the motive that was perplexing me. The thing that seemed to connect the two men was the Horseman's Guild... Or could it be just horses in general?

And, when I thought about it, the murder of the vet would surely rule out Mrs Douglas, and Torquil from the shooting party as well, since their issues were with Hamish, not Oliver.

Then I remembered that I'd said to Trinity I'd let the police know about the arguments in the pub. Pulling off the road into a lay-by, I dialled Dean's number, rehearsing a message in my head, since I expected to be answered by his voicemail.

But, surprisingly, Dean answered after only one ring. Quickly, I told him what Trinity had discovered about the altercations at The Queen's Arms, although I wasn't sure if they would be relevant to Mr Seaforth's murder.

"Thanks," he said, "we'll check those out." There was a pause. "We've got an urgent lead to follow up, so I'll need to catch up with you later, if that's okay. Can I pick you up, say, seven o'clock? We could go bowling."

Railroaded into a corner, I seemed to have no other option but to agree. "Can you make it seven thirty? I'm on my way to collect the mares, but I need to leave some contingency in case we get delayed."

"No problem. See you then." He rang off.

I stared at the road ahead for at least a minute before I started the lorry again and signalled to pull out. It looked like I had a date with Dean. But what about Craig?

———

I FOUND Craig looking perplexed in Hamish's old office in Balmoral, hands stuffed in his pockets. A thin layer of dust lay over everything, but otherwise it looked much as it had the first time I'd visited.

Jet scuffed across the wooden floor and put a paw on my foot, looking up at me with his soulful brown eyes. I put a hand on his head.

"What do I do with all this stuff?" Craig asked, waving an arm around the room.

"Maybe offer it to Mrs Douglas? Or is there an exhibition of estate history that might take some of it?" Flicking open the ledger on the desk, I added, "But some of this is stud information you'll need."

"Aye, of course. Sorry," he ran a hand through his hair, "it's just getting on top of me. I can't be doing with all the police questions and trying to get my head around the new job whilst still doing my old one."

"There's an easy answer to that. Advertise for a new Pony Boy."

"I couldnae be doing that."

"Why not? You're the boss now."

His face cleared. "You're right, you know. I'm sorry, I didnae sleep much last night and my head is mince."

The strengthening of his accent seemed to be a hint that Craig was feeling stressed. "How about us going for that coffee you suggested? This can wait."

"Aye. Just give me a minute to go wash my hands."

While I waited for him, I took the opportunity to examine Hamish's photos more closely, in particular the ones showing guild members.

Oliver Seaforth I quickly identified, standing proudly beside Hamish. Pat McDade was also there, and Will Thomson-Bond, our Glengowrie farrier. None of the other faces were ones I recognised. Pulling out my phone, I snapped a quick photo, just as Craig re-entered the room. He gave me a quizzical look.

"I can't help thinking that the Horseman's Guild is something to do with this," I explained. "Since both of them were members." I pointed at the photo. "Do you know any of these others?"

He pointed at a fat man in the back row. "Thon's Angus Hawksley who breeds Clydesdales. And beside him is Quentin Philpott the horse dealer." He indicated another. "I think that guy's a gentleman farmer whose wife runs the pony club, but I don't remember his name. And next to him is the back man."

"The Terminator?"

He nodded. "The very same. And Pat McDade you already know."

"And Will the farrier."

"Aye." He squinted at a man standing in shadow at the end

of the row. "I think that's George Reid the saddler, but it's hard to tell."

"Any of them have much to do with Hamish? Outside of the guild, I mean."

His lips pressed together. "The farrier comes here every week or two. And the saddler once or twice a year. We get our feed delivered from McDades. But that's about it."

"But you never heard any arguments or complaints?"

Craig shook his head. "Not that I can think of, sorry." He pointed at the door. "It'd be more comfortable to chat over coffee?"

———

THE BALMORAL CAFÉ WAS BUSY, it being the weekend, and we got what must've been the last free table. Placing his baseball cap beside him on the plastic tablecloth, Craig stirred his coffee thoughtfully. "I never got a chance to ask you," he said after a minute, "what did thon policeman want with you yesterday morning?"

"Oh," I looked down at my own coffee, hoping my cheeks weren't reddening, "they want me to investigate Hamish and Oliver's financial dealings. With my IT security business. You remember?"

"Aye. The dragon tattoo."

I made a face. "I call it Aye Spy Investigations." From a pocket in my phone case, I pulled out a card and handed it to him, rather than explain the spelling.

"IT security, digital forensics, social media vetting," he read, then looked up. "I suppose you've checked me out by now?"

My cheeks were definitely red this time. I shrugged. "It would've been silly of me not to. But I didn't find anything to worry about."

He thought on that for a moment. "Aye, I suppose you're right. Any lassie would be a fool not to check out some stranger she just met."

"Yeah, exactly."

"Did you check out thon farrier for Trinity? If he gets a clean report, I'll eat my hat."

My heart sank. "I never thought... to be honest, I've been so busy with the murder investigation it didn't cross my mind. But you're right, I should do. She's seeing him tonight."

He looked at me over the top of his Americano, then set it down again. "Why don't you stay up here tonight? We can go for dinner again. You can take the mares home tomorrow morning."

"Oh, I'm sorry, I can't, I've already made arrangements for this evening." I checked the time on my watch. "Actually, I'll need to get going soon, so I get back in time."

Craig sat back in his chair and stared at his coffee cup again. He seemed disappointed.

"Maybe next weekend?" I offered.

"Aye, okay." He drained his cup and stood up. "Let's go and get those mares loaded afore it gets too late."

CHAPTER SEVENTEEN

THE BOWLING ALLEY that Dean took me to that evening was a huge American-themed building in a retail park on the outskirts of Dundee.

Inside was noisy with the sound of skittles falling, balls bouncing in gutters and fruit machines pinging. Purple lights edged each lane with its highly polished wooden surface, and spotlights highlighted the triangular group of skittles at the end of each alley.

"I haven't played bowls for ages," I shouted in Dean's ear as we dropped our jackets over the seats in our lane.

He rubbed his hands and grinned. "Drinks are on the loser, then."

"That's okay," I countered. "You're driving and I'm not drinking. So that'll be lemonade all round."

"Unless you're a ringer, and you're just having me on?"

Suppressing a smile, I stepped over to the rack and selected a ball, testing it for weight. Seconds later it was rolling down the alley, off centre and slower than I'd have liked.

"Six!" crowed Dean as my score flashed onto the screen above us.

I rolled my shoulders and picked up my second ball. "Just getting my eye in."

Of course, Dean turned out to be a bit of an expert. If he didn't get a strike, he'd knock all the pins down with his second shot. But once he saw how useless I was, he started giving me hints and help.

At one point he put his arms round me from behind to show me how to aim. All I could smell was chocolate, and all I could feel was the warmth of his body behind me. It reminded me of that scene in the movie, *Ghost*, and my legs turned to jelly as his voice purred in my ear.

Then I became aware of something buzzing in my pocket, and the spell was broken. "My phone," I said apologetically, and fished it out.

Craig, the screen said, and I sat down heavily, waving at Dean to go and take his shot. "Hi Craig," I answered.

"Hi. Sorry to be bothering you, but I just found something out that I thought you should know. Or pass on to Trinity, anyway."

My heart stuttered. "Uh-huh?"

"That farrier, Richard Mortimer. He's married."

"Married! What's he doing asking Trinity out then?"

"Aye. You might well ask."

In the background, Dean sent his ball spinning down the alley at a rate of knots.

"Is that—are you at the bowling?" Craig asked in my ear.

"Strike!" Dean cried and punched the air.

"Wait, is that thon policeman?"

"I—it's just a work thing. He asked me here to discuss the murders."

"Work thing my elbow. He wants more than a discussion. I could see straight away he fancied you."

"I'm sure it's nothing like that," I spluttered.

"No wonder you couldnae do dinner wi' me th' night."

"I'm sorry, it was already—"

"An' you can forget dinner wi' me next week an' all." He slammed the phone down.

I sat back in my seat, momentarily stunned. My eyes stung, and my throat felt like it was burning, so I reached for my drink and took a gulp, then nearly spat it all out again when Dean sat down next to me.

"Everything okay?" he asked.

Pulling a tissue out of my pocket, I wiped my mouth to play for time while I tried to gather my scattered thoughts. "Uh, I'm not sure. I—I need to phone Trinity. Sorry."

Quirking an eyebrow, he stood again. "Okay, I'll give you some privacy."

"Thanks," I said, even as my fingers were punching her number.

Dean sauntered off in the direction of the toilets.

"Izzy!" Trinity answered. "You having a good time, girl?" I could almost hear her frown. "Or are you looking for an excuse to leave?"

"No, it's fine—"

"Great. Look at this," she turned video mode on, and something blurry flashed across the screen. "We went back to Richard's. He's got all these cool animals." She pointed the screen, and the picture sharpened to show something that looked like a fish tank. "Well, reptiles. This one's a python." She zoomed in on the vivarium and the leopard-like markings of a large snake swam into view.

I gasped, as some pennies began to drop. Snakes were long and thin. In his vision, Eagle saw something long and thin. More clues fell into place, like how he'd disappeared from the pub the night Hamish was killed, and how there were stepping stones from there, across the river, and into the

Balmoral estate. "Trin, do you know, does he have any spiders?"

"I dunno. Hang on, I'll ask him," then her voice slowed, as if she'd just started to catch on to what I was thinking, "he's just come back in."

"No!" I almost screamed. "Don't," I hissed, "play dumb. Be nice. Play along. We'll come and get you."

"What's that you want to ask, darlin'?" I heard Richard's voice in the background.

My mind raced. "Tell him you need to know the address to book a taxi."

While she asked, I frantically scanned the bowling alley, hunting for Dean. But there was no sign of him.

On the phone, Richard was saying, "You don't need a taxi, darlin', I'll take you home."

"O—okay," she replied, then spoke into the phone. "Thank you, but I won't be needing a taxi after all."

"Just sit tight," I told her, "we'll find you—" but she'd disconnected.

My pulse was hammering now. *Where's Dean?* In desperation, I dialled his number. "Dean, we need to go. Trinity's in danger. I'll grab your coat and meet you at the front door."

Give him his due, he didn't argue, and a few seconds later we were hurrying out to his car.

CHAPTER EIGHTEEN

"SAY AGAIN?" Dean said as we jumped into his car.

"I think Richard Mortimer the farrier is the killer."

The policeman's brow creased. "Why?"

"Before we get into that, can you track down his address from police records or something? I think it's here in Dundee somewhere. Trinity is with him."

He gave me a concerned look and phoned it in.

While he did that, I was busy interrogating Google on my mobile, trying to track the man down. My stomach was in knots. If he got at all suspicious of Trinity—and I wasn't sure how good her acting skills would be, seeing as she seemed to have put two and two together—it could all be too late by the time we got there.

Dean finished his call and put his phone in the centre console.

"Should we head for the centre?" I suggested. "Then maybe we'd be closer to wherever he lives?"

He jerked his chin and put the car into gear. "He might live on the outskirts. I'll wait at the entrance to the retail park. They shouldn't take long getting back to me. Now, tell me why you suspect him?"

"He's got pet snakes. And I think he probably has spiders too." I remembered the snakeskin cowboy boots. "He left the pub the night Hamish was killed, and he could've gone back into the estate. Plus, he seems the type."

Dean didn't try to hide the cynicism in his voice. "Just because you don't like someone's hobbies, it doesn't make them a killer."

"How about—" I thought fast, "—he put the spider in Hamish's boot, and hid outside where he wouldn't be seen." Into my head swam the picture Eagle had given me of the shadowy figure in the brimmed hat. *A stetson?* "When the spider bite didn't work, Richard followed Hamish to the stable, and scared Eagle with a snake, so Hamish got knocked down and kicked."

Dean pressed his lips together as he parked us at the slip to the ring road. "Far-fetched. But plausible. But that doesn't explain the vet's death. Or *why* Richard would kill Hamish."

He had a point. I wracked my brains, skimming through the clues I'd discovered like a computer scrolling through data. "The guild!" Inspiration struck. "Maybe he was the one whose membership application got rejected. I saw him sucking up to Oliver at the pub. Maybe he saw Hamish as a stumbling block, and that's why the man got killed."

"Hmmm. I can see why they might not want an over-confident Londoner in their midst."

I looked across at him, my mouth hanging open. *London.* Of course. Suddenly, the remaining pieces fell into place, and I jabbed frantically at the keypad on my phone, speaking quickly as I did so. "Oliver is a vet. He would know Richard kept reptiles. Or maybe he just discovered that fact, maybe Richard took a snake to the surgery after hours, and mentioned about spiders. And the vet connected the dots, so he had to be killed."

This earned me another sceptical look. "All because he couldn't get into a secret society?"

"People have killed for a lot less," I said, remembering the fiction plots again.

Dean's phone chirruped, and he snatched it up. "Yes?" He listened carefully, then put the car into gear and drove off. "Old Glamis Road. Not far."

"C'mon, c'mon." I stared at the screen on my phone, willing it to work faster.

"I'm driving as fast as I can, Izzy."

"Not you—ah! Yes! Here it is." I punched the air in triumph, like a jockey winning the Grand National for the first time. "Family tree records show that Richard Mortimer was born in London, and that his father was Marcus Serjeant. The guy who tried to shoot the Queen." It all made sense now. "Richard was out for revenge on the man who thwarted his father's bid for fame and got him locked up in an institution."

Dean's face was grim. "I'll call for backup."

"No, wait, that might get Trinity killed. Can we try the nice way first? Say..." my thoughts raced, "We were in the area and... I got a call that a horse is sick and I need her help?"

He puffed out a breath. "It might work. But I'll get them on their way." Picking up his phone, he punched a button and called for help. This probably wasn't the time to remind him about it being against the law to speak on the phone while driving.

Seconds later, we drew up outside a nondescript semi-detached house, and I almost fell out of the passenger door in my haste to get to Trinity.

Dean was already opening the garden gate and ushered me in. "You're on," he said. "I'll back you up if need be."

The doorbell chimed somewhere inside the house and I hopped on one leg as I waited. It seemed to take forever, but finally the door swung open, revealing the farrier in his customary black outfit.

"Hi, sorry to bother you, Richard, I'm looking for Trinity. One of the horses is sick and I need her help." If my face showed the worry I was feeling, I hoped he'd think it was concern for the horse.

He wiped the back of his hand across his forehead. "You're too late, darlin'. She already left."

"Oh, I thought you were going to give her a lift home?"

"I was. But she said she had to go, and then she went and jumped in a taxi."

I had to work hard to keep my teeth from grinding. There was no way she'd ordered a taxi in the short space of time since I spoke to her—especially since she didn't appear to even know the address he was at.

"Okay, mate, thanks." Dean took my arm in a strong grip and turned for the gate. "Let's get you home, Izzy, so you can look after that horse," he said in an over-loud voice. For a second, I contemplated arguing, but Dean hissed at me like a ventriloquist. "Wait!"

By the time we got to the car, Richard had disappeared back inside, the knots in my stomach had turned into macrame, and Dean's face was carved in stone.

"Sorry for hustling you away like that," he said, "but we're in a potential hostage or kidnap situation now. We need to wait for the backup." He started the car.

"I'll try phoning her," I said, pulling the handset from my pocket as I clambered into the passenger seat. Then I yelped in fright as something darted across my peripheral vision.

The back door opened, and Dean spun round angrily. "Stop right there or I'll..."

"It's just me!" From the rear seat, Trinity raised her hands like the baddie in a cowboy movie, her chest heaving.

I almost cried with relief. "How did you get out?"

"Through the garden. And over a fence. He left a ventilation window open in his reptile shed. He's—"

The front door of the house burst open, and Richard charged out, brandishing a machete.

Dean took one look at him and floored the accelerator.

In the distance I could hear police sirens, and as I peered out the back window of the car, I saw squad cars screeching to a halt outside the house and burly policemen with tasers overpowering the farrier. My clenched fists relaxed. "They got him."

"You sure?" Dean glanced at me quickly.

"Yeah."

He did a u-turn and went back to report to the officers outside Richard's house. "Wait there till I check the status," he said, and jumped out.

I put my arm between the seats and clasped Trinity's hand. "You okay?"

"A bit shaken, if I'm honest. But not stirred." Her breathing was getting back to normal.

"I'm just glad you're okay. And that you managed to escape."

She nodded. "Had me a bit of luck there." She made a face. "But I wish I'd never agreed to go out with the man. He's a weirdo. Has all these John Wayne posters everywhere, and then these sheds of animals in his back garden."

"You dodged a bullet with that one."

Her peal of laughter was like music to my ears. "I see what you did there."

I grinned. "But if you hadn't gone out with him, I'd never have worked out he was the killer."

"You really think he is?"

I nodded. "He's Marcus Serjeant's son."

"Never?"

"Yep. Hopefully the police will find more evidence, now they've got a proper suspect."

"An' at least Craig's off the hook."

Craig. My face fell. I'd been so intent on rescuing Trinity that I'd forgotten how royally I'd messed things up with him. He'd never speak to me again.

A little bit of my heart died inside.

———

IT WAS the early hours of Sunday morning before a squad car dropped me and Trinity back at the cottage.

Worn out from all the questions, we opened the front door to let Jorja out, and stumbled round the stable yard, quickly checking all the horses. Then we clambered up the stairs, too tired to speak.

I fell in a heap on my bed, fully clothed, and Jorja leapt up beside me, snuggling in. "You're not supposed to be here, your bed's downstairs," I whispered to her. But I was too exhausted to make her leave. Instead, I gave her a hug. She squirmed closer. "I wish you were Craig," I muttered, tears pricking at my eyelids.

How was I ever going to fix things with him?

When I looked back at the times we'd spent together, I could see how good he'd been to me—buying me soup when I was recovering from Eagle's vision, rescuing me from Richard's attentions in the pub, and then keeping me company over dinner. And he'd made me laugh.

Yet all I'd done was be suspicious of him, thinking he might have killed Hamish, even though I'd ruled out all the motives, and thinking he was a philanderer, only because of what Pat McDade said. A tear rolled down my cheek and I swiped it away. Really, I didn't deserve him.

And maybe some things just couldn't be fixed.

But there was a lesson for me to learn here, something positive to take from the mess I'd made with Craig. Kicking off my shoes, I pulled the blankets over me and cuddled Jorja closer.

Next time—if there ever was a next time—I'd take Trinity's advice to heart, and learn to be better at showing what I felt. Or even just *letting* myself feel things. Locking my heart away was all very well, but look where it'd got me with Craig? Nowhere. Absolutely nowhere.

As my head sank into the pillow and sleep finally overtook me, I made a resolution. I would try to show my feelings more, and let the people I cared about know that they were important to me. That couldn't be so difficult, could it?

CHAPTER NINETEEN

RAIN DRUMMED on the slate roof of the cottage as I stumbled downstairs the next morning. Outside, everything was grey, and it matched my mood.

Flicking the kettle on, I yawned and rubbed my eyes, which felt like they had half of Portobello beach in them.

The front door swung open and Trinity came in, shedding a dripping overcoat and hanging it on a hook by the door. "Morning, boss," she greeted me.

I didn't have the energy to tell her for the hundredth time not to call me that.

"That's all the horses sorted. And Eagle is keeping Allegra and Daisy entertained." She raised an eyebrow. "Now, grab your coat while I change my boots. I'm taking you out for breakfast. It's our day off today."

I groaned. "Not sure I can eat anything."

"Coffee, then." She held out my coat. "My treat."

A short time later, at one of the cherry-red tables in Kaffe Kalista, I had my hands warming on a massive cup of cappuccino.

Trinity placed a blueberry muffin in front of me. "Eat that. You need some carbs."

Over by the window, the misses Large were in full flow.

"Tried to kill the Queen, he did, back when he was part of the household calorie."

"The Household Cavalry, aye, that's the one."

"And then he tries to kill that wee lassie. The one who's the saucy dancing teacher."

"Salsa dancing, aye."

I jerked a thumb at the spinsters. "You should go set them right, Trin. Make friends. Cultivate your sources."

She glanced at the door, then shrugged. "Okay." Picking up her herbal tea, she made her way over to their table.

I watched her go, surprised that she hadn't argued. Then, with a shrug, I turned my attention to my coffee. And the muffin. *Maybe just a bite,* I thought, breaking off a little piece and tasting it tentatively. In the background, a bell pinged, but I was oblivious. I took another bite. *Delicious.* My flatmate was right. I needed carbs.

"Morning."

I startled, then, slowly, my eyes travelled upwards, tracking from the cake on the plate before me to black jeans, then a grey v-neck jersey, dark stubble, and finally—brown eyes. Those melting chocolate eyes. "Dean."

Putting a rain-speckled leather jacket over the back of the chair opposite me, he sat down, and somehow a coffee appeared in front of him. "Looks like we'll get Richard put away for Hamish's murder. Thanks to you."

I nodded. I didn't trust myself to speak just yet.

"Heard this morning that I'm getting a special commendation for my part in solving the crime. It should stand me in good stead for the detective exam. Also thanks to you."

All this praise was making me blush. "That's good news."

He swallowed. "But I think you deserve more than just

thanks. Maybe a slap-up afternoon tea at one of the fancy hotels in Perth? Or even Gleneagles if you don't mind the longer drive?"

My eyes widened. *Didn't see that coming.* I picked up my cappuccino to gain some thinking time. Last time I'd been out with the copper it had ended with Craig finding out and me almost in tears. My chest constricted. Did I want to risk it again?

Then my phone buzzed. "'Scuse me," I said, and swiped it open.

> Craig: *I'm getting sent to Windsor to cover for the stable manager there. He got injured. Queen says to keep Eagle at Glengowrie for now. She'll pay. Bye.*

Rocking back in my chair, I stared at the screen. *Craig is going to England. Almost as far away from here as he could get.* And he hadn't sent an X at the end of his text message. Which pretty much confirmed that there was no way I'd be able to fix things with him now, even with my new resolution to be more open and better at sharing my feelings. I sighed.

> Me: *Thanks for letting me know. That sounds like a good opportunity. All the best.*

"Everything okay?" Dean's voice was gravelly.

Blinking hard, I glanced over at the window table, relieved to see that Trinity was keeping the ladies occupied, her face animated and her hands waving as she described the events of yesterday. Nobody was eavesdropping on our conversation. "Yeah, just a client."

Dean raised his cup to his lips, and met my eyes over the top. "So. Gleneagles?"

It was undeniable, he really was very dishy. The epitome of the tall, dark and handsome stranger. And he was good company, even though I'd not felt the same connection with him as I did with Craig. Perhaps if I spent more time with him, he'd open up to me and share more about himself, be less of a stranger?

I shrugged. "Why not?" It would be exciting. And I'd get to know Dean better.

Life up here was turning out to be pretty exciting as well. In the space of three days I'd met the Queen, been interviewed for the paper, solved a murder, and now I was going for the very first time to what was probably the fanciest hotel in Scotland. Whoever was it that said things in a Highland village would be boring?

Not me.

―――

THE END

―――

Want to read more *about Izzy and Trinity, and the mysteries they encounter in the Highlands of Scotland?*
Order the next book, **A Right Royal Revenge**:

A NOTE FROM THE AUTHOR

As I wrote the final chapters of this novel, the coronavirus pandemic became more and more of an issue in daily life.

Escaping into Izzy's world was a wonderful antidote for me—and I hope it has been for you too. Stay safe, stay well, and I hope to see you soon for some more Scottish cozy mysteries!

THE HIGHLAND HORSE WHISPERER SERIES

Sign up to my newsletter to be the first to find out about special offers, and when the next book will be available:

rozmarshall.co.uk/newsletter,

or find the series—and my other books—at:

rozmarshall.co.uk/books.

ALSO BY R.B. MARSHALL

The **Highland Horse Whisperer** series

Cozy Mystery set in Scotland (and London for the prequel):

- The Secret Santa Mystery
- A Corpse at the Castle
- A Right Royal Revenge (releasing 30 Nov 2020)
- A Henchman at the Highland Games (due 2021)

WRITING AS ROZ MARSHALL:

The **Celtic Fey** series

Urban Fantasy / Young Adult Fantasy set in Scotland (and the faerie realm):

- Unicorn Magic
- Kelpie Curse
- Faerie Quest
- The Fey Bard
- Merlin's Army (due early 2021)
- The Celtic Fey (Books 1-3. Also in paperback)

Secrets in the Snow series

Sports Romance / Women's Fiction set in a Scottish ski school:

- Fear of Falling
- My Snowy Valentine
- The Racer Trials
- Snow Blind
- Weathering the Storm

Half Way Home stories

Young Adult Science Fiction set in Hugh Howey's *Half Way Home* universe:

- Nobody's Hero
- The Final Solution

Scottish stories:

- Still Waters

WRITING AS BELLE MCINNES:

Mary's Ladies series

Scottish Historical Romance telling the story of Mary Queen of Scots:

- *A Love Divided*
- *A Love Beyond*
- *A Love Concealed*

FROM THE AUTHOR

Fact and Fiction

As much as I can, I like to base the locations and history in my books on real places and events, adding my fictional elements around them.

ROYAL HISTORY

Back in 1981, a seventeen-year-old called Marcus Sarjeant fired six shots at the Queen during the Trooping the Colour parade, before he was overcome by a guardsman and the police.

I mixed historical fact and fiction by making Hamish one of the brave souls who took Marcus down, with the stud manager's job being his reward.

In reality, the Queen's Highland Pony stud at Balmoral is (currently) run by a lady who is part of a family with great expertise with that breed, but I wanted to make the story very obviously not about her and her family.

LOCATION, LOCATION, LOCATION

Glengowrie village is fictitious, but is based on a couple of real villages in Perthshire. Glengowrie House and the Letham family are also fictitious, but similar mansions and families exist throughout Scotland!

Balmoral Castle is obviously a real place, but my descriptions of the stables there are purely a product of my imagination, based on stable blocks I've seen or visited at other stately homes.

I hope this blend of fact and fiction makes for a believable story without offending any real people or villages!

THE HORSEMAN'S GUILD

Rumour has it that 'The Horseman's Word', a secret society/trade guild, exists and thrives in the north-east of Scotland. As Craig says in the story, they are said to have a special word they can use to calm any horse.

I personally have no experience of it—as I live in the south-east—so everything about the guild in this story is pure fiction and conjecture.

ABOUT THE AUTHOR

Like my amateur sleuth, Izzy, I'm a Scottish, dressage riding, computer geek who loves coffee—but there the similarity ends. She is far smarter than me, and a lot younger!

I hope you'll join me in discovering where her curiosity leads to next...

Get the next book: **A Right Royal Revenge**

I ALSO WRITE IN OTHER GENRES:

Fantasy and clean romance/women's fiction, as Roz Marshall: rozmarshall.co.uk/books

Historical Romance, telling the story of Mary Queen of Scots, as Belle McInnes: books2read.com/rl/MarysLadies

Here's where you'll find me:
rozmarshall.co.uk/books

facebook.com/rozmarshallauthor

GLOSSARY

Argy-bargy: Heated argument

Bay (horse): A brown horse with black legs, black mane and tail

Black pudding: A Scottish delicacy, made from oatmeal, spices and pork offal

Breeches: Riding leg wear, shorter at the ankle to fit better under long boots. See **jodhpurs**

Chestnut (horse): A golden-red coloured horse

Copper: Slang word for a policeman

Cover (a mare): When a stallion mates with a female horse

Cranachan: A traditional Scottish dessert, made from cream, raspberries, oats and whisky

Dark web: A part of the **deep web**, consisting of secret networks that can only be accessed using special software or specific authorisation

Deep web: A part of the internet containing websites or apps which cannot be found by regular search engines such as Google

Dressage: The training and gymnasticising of horses. Also used to describe the competitions where the results of that training are demonstrated

Dun: A horse colour, where the body is fawn or brown coloured and the mane, tail, and lower legs are black

Farrier: A person qualified to shoe horses

Freemasons: Secretive organisations or clubs that trace their origins to tradesmen's fraternities from the end of the fourteenth century

(The) Fuzz: The police

Gamie: Gamekeeper

Garron: A sturdy pony used for transporting deer carcases, usually a Highland Pony

Gelding: A castrated male horse

Gilet: A light sleeveless padded jacket or vest, also called a body warmer

Grey (horse): A horse colour, varying from steel-grey to white, sometimes dapple grey

Guinness: Irish beer. Dark, almost black

Guns: Weapons; also a collective name for the participants in a shoot, eg a deer hunt

Hack: A trail ride in the countryside

Highland Pony: Breed of pony native to Scotland. Sturdy and trustworthy, usually dun or grey in colour

Horsemanship: The training of horses using 'natural' methods such as body language. Sometimes called 'Natural Horsemanship'

Horse Whisperer: See **Horsemanship**. Also refers to a horse psychic, who can 'speak' to horses, or 'listen' to them and report the conversations to the owner

Household Cavalry: A mounted British army regiment that carries out ceremonial duties on State and Royal occasions, including the provision of a Sovereign's Escort, most commonly seen on The Queen's Birthday Parade (Trooping the Colour) in June each year

In his cups: Drunk

IT: Information Technology

Jobsworth: Someone who sticks to the rules. "It's more than my job's worth to do that..."

Jodhpurs (jods): Riding leg wear, designed to be worn with ankle (jodhpur) boots

Keep cup: A reusable coffee cup

Landrover (Landy): A British brand of four-wheel drive car, rugged and utilitarian

Lorry: Truck

Lunge (a horse): Exercise a horse by moving it in a circle around you, on the end of a long rope (lunge rein or lunge line)

Mobile Phone: Cellphone

Natural Horsemanship: See **Horsemanship**

Ne'er-do-well (never do well): A person who is up to no good. A rogue

Ozzie: Australian

PC: Police Constable

Pleb: From *plebeian*. A commoner

Round pen: A round enclosure used for horse training, usually fenced in wood or metal hurdles

Rozzer: Cockney slang for a policeman

Rug: Horse blanket used to keep them warm and dry in inclement weather

Sassenach: Scots word for an English person

Shenanigans: High jinks, mischief

Skedaddle: Hurry, scurry

Skewbald: A brown & white horse, also called tobiano

Sports horse: A type of horse, usually a cross between a **warmblood** or **thoroughbred** and a native breed of horse or pony. Versatile for jumping or dressage

Stable: The stall or loose box where a horse is housed (if necessary)

Stables: Either a row of individual stables, or sometimes the whole establishment

Stable Yard: A facility for horses, usually including **stables** and paddocks plus riding arena(s). Sometimes part of a farm or stately home, or sometimes purpose-built. Abbreviated to '**Yard**'

Tack: Horse equipment, usually the leatherwork such as saddle and bridle

Tattersall: Chequered fabric

Tenner: Ten pound (GBP) note. Money

Thon: Scots word for *that* or *those*

Thoroughbred: A breed of horse originating in England and specialising in racing

Two shakes (of a lamb's tail): Quickly, in no time

Warmblood: A type of horse, originally a cross between thoroughbreds and European draft (cart) horses, but now specialising mainly in dressage

Wellington Boots (wellies): Waterproof rubber boots

Yard: See **Stable Yard**

CHARACTERS

Izzy Paterson: Horse trainer for Glengowrie stud, and proprietor of *Aye Spy Investigations*

Lady Alice Letham: Izzy's boss, and owner of Glengowrie House and stud

Beverly Douglas: Hamish's wife

Craig MacDonald: Pony Boy/Assistant Stud Manager at Balmoral

Sergeant Dean Lovell: Local policeman

Dev (Devlin) Connolly: Izzy's ex-colleague and consultant in *Aye Spy Investigations*

Edie (Edith) Large: Spinster sister from Glengowrie

Evan Grainger: Glengowrie postman

Francine McDade: Pat's wife

Gail Fisher: Stan's wife

Gremlin: A computer program written by Izzy which searches the deep web

Hamish Douglas: Stud Manager at Balmoral

Ina (Thomasina) Large: Spinster sister from Glengowrie

Jet: Craig's black Labrador

Jimmy Harkin: Lady Letham's handyman. Husband of Ursula, the cook/housekeeper

Jorja: The lost Jack Russell terrier

Kalista Dudek: Polish owner of the coffee shop in Glengowrie

Laura Douglas: Hamish and Beverly's daughter

Leo: Izzy's dressage horse

Neil Etherington: Reporter for the Gowrie Gazette

Miles Ainsworth: Gamekeeper at Balmoral

Mrs Muriel Beaton: Owner of the Riverside Guest House B&B near Balmoral

Oliver Seaforth: Local vet

Patrick (Pat) McDade: Owner/manager of a chain of agricultural food stores

Richard Mortimer: Farrier

Stan Fisher: Stud groom at Balmoral

The Terminator: The 'back man' (I'll be back). Horse chiropractor

Torquil: Member of the shooting party

Trinity Allen: Izzy's friend and colleague

Ursula Harkin: Lady Letham's cook and housekeeper. Jimmy's wife

Constable Vicky Adamson: Policewoman

Will Thomson-Bond: Glengowrie farrier

Zak Carpenter: Ozzie barman at The Queen's Arms

RECIPE 1: SWEET POTATO STEW

Ginger, sweet potato and coconut milk stew with lentils and kale

This sweet potato and coconut milk stew is a glowing and mellow shade of orange with big, vibrant pops of green from kale and cilantro.

Find the recipe here (scroll down the page):
https://thefirstmess.com/2020/02/19/sweet-potato-coconut-milk-stew/

RECIPE 2: LEEK & SWEET POTATO SOUP

Perfect on a cold winter's day, this soup is quick to make and really tasty to eat!

Find the recipe here:

https://www.bbcgoodfood.com/user/107145/recipe/leek-sweet-potato-soup

ACKNOWLEDGMENTS

Thank you to Mairi, Angie and Liz, my beta-reading and editing team, who added extra polish and value to my scribblings. Also grateful thanks to Gillian for her input on Scottish Police procedures!